"Kiss me, Mariella."

Their gazes held for a second. Luca was waiting for her, she realized. He understood she'd been hurt and he was letting her make the first move. It was unexpected. She was used to him bossing her around. Now he was giving her the power, and it made him even more difficult to resist.

She leaned into his hand, tilted up her face, and with her heart in her throat touched her lips to his. The connection between them was so strong it rocked her core.

For the first time since leaving her old life behind, she threw caution to the wind, wrapping her arms around his torso and pulling him closer.

The moment she did it, everything changed.

Dear Reader,

For nearly twelve years I lived in Alberta, Canada, with my husband and children. My mom would come to visit us annually, and her visit always included a trip to the Rocky Mountains and, more often than not, lunch at the fabulously decadent Banff Springs Hotel. I always thought there was something magical about it. It's perched at the pinnacle of town, a great stone castle looking up at Cascade Mountain and down the Bow River Valley. The food is excellent; the atmosphere even better. When I thought of putting a heroine somewhere to reclaim her life, the townsite of Banff simply fitted the bill.

Of course I needed a hotel, and a to-die-for-handsome hero. I found him in Italian Luca Fiori. Luca is heir to the Fiori hotel empire, and is sent to Banff to oversee the newest company acquisition, the Fiori Cascade. The Cascade is a place for relaxation and rejuvenation, for a bit of decadence and specialness. Luca says it is to "remember the romance."

As I write this letter, I've just returned home from a wedding… my mom's wedding. After she spent many years on her own, I couldn't be happier that she "remembered the romance" and that she and her new husband "found" each other—again. Nearly sixty years ago they dated as teenagers…and now here they are, newlyweds. By the time this book hits the shelves, they will be getting close to celebrating their first wedding anniversary.

Maybe there's magic in the number sixty. Because this year Harlequin is celebrating its sixtieth birthday. It's so very special to me both as an author and as a Canadian to be part of Harlequin's tradition of outstanding romance fiction.

Why not celebrate Harlequin's diamond birthday with me? I'd love to hear from you. You can e-mail me at donna@donnaalward.com.

With my very best wishes,

Donna

DONNA ALWARD

Hired: The Italian's Bride

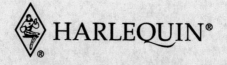

HARLEQUIN®

TORONTO • NEW YORK • LONDON
AMSTERDAM • PARIS • SYDNEY • HAMBURG
STOCKHOLM • ATHENS • TOKYO • MILAN • MADRID
PRAGUE • WARSAW • BUDAPEST • AUCKLAND

For Mum and Harold

Recycling programs
for this product may
not exist in your area.

ISBN-13: 978-0-373-18450-7

HIRED: THE ITALIAN'S BRIDE

First North American Publication 2009.

Copyright © 2009 by Donna Alward.

www.eHarlequin.com

Printed in U.S.A.

A busy wife and mother of three (two daughters and the family dog), **Donna Alward** believes hers is the best job in the world: a combination of stay-at-home mom and romance novelist. An avid reader since childhood, Donna always made up her own stories. She completed her arts degree in English literature in 1994, but it wasn't until 2001 that she penned her first full-length novel and found herself hooked on writing romance. In 2006 she sold her first manuscript, and now writes warm, emotional stories for the Harlequin Romance line.

Donna loves being back on the east coast of Canada— and in her new home office in Nova Scotia—after nearly twelve years in Alberta, where she began her career writing about cowboys and the West. Donna's debut novel for the Harlequin Romance series, *Hired by the Cowboy,* was awarded the Booksellers Best Award in 2008 for Best Traditional Romance.

With the Atlantic Ocean only minutes from her doorstep, Donna has found a fresh take on life and promises even more great romances in the near future!

Donna loves to hear from readers.
You can contact her through her Web site at www.donnaalward.com or visit her MySpace page at www.myspace.com/dalward.

In November, queen of the rugged rancher
Patricia Thayer and sparkling new talent
Donna Alward team up to bring you an
extraspecial Christmas treat—
two stories in one volume for double the romance!

Montana, Mistletoe, Marriage

Join sisters Amelia and Kelley for Christmas at
Rocking H Ranch, where these feisty cowgirls swap
presents for proposals, mistletoe for marriage, and
experience the unbeatable rush of falling in love.

Praise for Patricia Thayer:

"Patricia Thayer offers readers
a rich reading experience with emotional power,
fresh characters and passion."
—*Romantic Times BOOKreviews*

Praise for Donna Alward:

"Talented Donna Alward weaves a
gorgeous secluded setting, intense
suspenseful plot and well developed characters
into a most rewarding read."
—*Cataromance.com*

*And don't forget to look out for Christmas extras
at the end of each story!*

CHAPTER ONE

"Ms. Ross? Mr. Fiori has arrived."

He was here.

"Thank you, Becky. Show him in."

Mari ran a hand over her already smooth hair, trying hard not to resent a man she'd never met. Luca Fiori, golden son of the Fiori Resort empire. Rich, powerful, and according to her online research, a bit of a playboy.

Just what she—and the hotel—needed. Not.

She could just make out the sound of his voice, smooth and warm, coming from the reception area. The sound sent a flutter through her tummy. Becky would be bringing him back any moment. Perhaps she should go out to meet him. Yes, that would probably be the genial, professional thing to do. But her feet wouldn't move. Instead she turned her head to both sides, assessing the office as if through a stranger's eyes. Her new office, though she couldn't help feeling a bit of an interloper. What Fiori needed to see was a woman confident in her new position.

Even if she wasn't, she had to give that appearance. She made sure everything was in its place. Not a speck of dust or scrap of paper. Everything had to be perfect. The only thing that revealed she'd even been there that morning was her mug, half-full of cold tea, a faint half-moon of lipstick marring the cream-colored ceramic.

Mari inhaled, then let it out slowly, trying to relax her shoulders. She carried all her tension there and right now they were sitting close to her ears, she was so nervous. She pushed them down and attempted a smile. She had to show him she was up to the job…the job she'd had for exactly two weeks and three days.

Seconds later Becky returned, extending a hand and showing Luca into the office.

All Mari's practiced greetings flew out of her head. "Mr. Fiori."

The pictures didn't do him justice, she realized, as her heart gave a definitive *thud*. He was taller than he seemed from the online pictures. He was wearing a suit, but with such a casual flair she wasn't sure it actually could be called a suit at all. Black trousers and shoes and a white shirt, open at the collar, with a black jacket worn carelessly over top. The unbuttoned collar revealed a slice of tanned skin and she saw his hand tuck into his trouser pocket just before she lifted her eyes to his face.

She'd been caught assessing. His twinkling eyes

told her so and the crooked, cocky smile confirmed it. Her cheeks flushed as her gaze skittered away.

"Ms. Ross, the acting manager, I presume?"

She wet her lips and pasted on a smile, trying hard to ignore the heat that blossomed anew in her face at the sound of his smooth, rich voice. She extended her hand. "Yes. Welcome to the Bow Valley Inn."

"You mean the Fiori Cascade."

Mari went cold. Of course. She'd received the memo about the name change and had simply forgotten it in her nervousness. She looked up at Luca's mouth. He was smiling, at least, not angry with her for the slip.

She pulled her hand out of his, attempting to keep the polite turn of her lips in place. "Yes, of course. Old habits." She gestured to a small seating area. "Come in and sit down. I'll ask Becky for some refreshment."

"Why don't we go to the lounge, instead?" He raised one eyebrow at her. "I passed one as I came through the lobby. It'll help give me a feel of the place. And the lounge will be much more intimate, don't you think?"

Mari's hand froze on the handset of the phone. This wasn't what she'd planned. Her pulse drummed at the word "intimate." She'd wanted coffee and the chef's signature scones, followed by a brief presentation of what she considered the Inn's finest points and some basic proposals for changes and upgrades. She'd spent hours getting it the way she wanted—

flawless. And with an appropriate amount of distance between them.

"Is something wrong, Ms. Ross?"

She rubbed her lips together. "No, not at all." Her voice came out thin and reedy and she cleared her throat, stretching her lips in a smile again. "Coffee in the Athabasca Room would be fine." She'd simply have to remember what she'd put in her report and make her points as they went along.

"I look forward to hearing your ideas. Perhaps you'd take me on a tour later?" He stepped aside, letting her exit first. His voice was smooth, his smile charming. Mari exhaled again, trying to keep her shoulders down. She could do this. She wasn't used to thinking on her feet, but she could do it. She'd just ignore what she knew about his reputation. Or the fact that he fairly exuded charm without even trying.

The lounge was nearly empty at ten in the morning. Two other couples sat at tables, sipping from large mugs and chatting quietly. Mari led him past the main bar to a smaller corner one, perching on one of the backed stools, making sure there were several inches between them. Luca took the seat next to her and the scent of his expensive cologne reached her nose. There was no mistaking the confident ease with which he carried himself. This was a man completely out of her league. Not that she was looking. She wasn't even close to looking, not when the very thought of any physical contact with a man sent chills down her spine.

"This might be my favorite view in the whole hotel," she began, focusing on her job, determined he see the Inn...the Cascade...at its best. The way she was turned, she could look out over the hotel front grounds and down over the valley, the turquoise-blue of the Bow River a shining snake through the gold and green hues of autumn. "And our coffee is superior. We import it from—"

"The scenery *is* spectacular." He interrupted her and she realized that he wasn't looking at the view at all, but at her. Nerves tumbled in her stomach and her voice trailed off, unsure of how to continue. He must think her provincial, not the standard of management *Fiori* employed. Certainly not up to bantering, like he seemed to expect.

Mari turned back to the bar and put her hand on the coffeepot that was set out. It didn't matter. This was her job and she wanted to keep it. Wanted it more than anything else in the world.

"Coffee, Mr. Fiori?"

She looked up when he remained silent and their eyes met.

Her hand shook on the handle of the pot. He was watching her steadily, so unwavering that tightness cinched her chest. She willed it away, telling herself it was his power as her boss that had her so unsettled. It wasn't his fault that he was so handsome. Wasn't his fault that his eyes were the color of melted molasses toffee, only a slightly deeper shade than his hair. He wasn't responsible for the perfectly shaped lips, either, or the way he spoke, with flawless inflection and just a hint of Italian accent. He was possibly more magnetic than he was in the pictures on the computer or in the industry magazines she kept filed on her bookshelf. She would imagine he got his way often simply from his looks and charm. But not here, not with her. There were important things at stake.

"Call me Luca, please," he answered finally.

She forced herself to pour the coffee as the waitress returned with a basket of warm scones. "Luca, then."

"You're not going to tell me your first name."

She raised an eyebrow, cautiously determined not to let him ride roughshod over her. "You own this hotel. Don't you know it already?"

He laughed, the sound devoid of any pretence. A genuine laugh that nearly warmed her from the inside out. "Remind me, then."

A smile crept up her lips; she couldn't help it. She'd expected him to be practiced, but the truth was everything about him was natural. From the way he wore his clothes to his manners to his easy chuckle. There was nothing fake about Luca Fiori. His charm was innate and genuine.

And therein lay the danger, she realized. In her books, charm equaled trouble. She didn't need trouble. In any form.

"Mari. My first name is Mari."

"Oh, Mari, I believe you've short-changed me."

She picked up a spoon and stirred sugar—a heaping teaspoon of it—into her coffee. "Short-changed you? How?"

"Because I know your name is really Mariella."

Her fingers gripped the spoon. She much preferred Mari now. She'd been Mari ever since moving to Banff three years ago. No more Mariella. Mariella had been scared and obedient and faceless. She hadn't been a person at all.

"I go by Mari. Or you may continue calling me Ms. Ross." She didn't even attempt to keep the cool out of her voice.

Luca split a scone and buttered it. "Mariella is a lovely Italian name. It means *beloved*."

"I know what it means."

Undaunted, he continued. "It was also my grandmother's name."

Mari swallowed a mouthful of coffee too fast and it burned all the way down her throat. His grandmother's name wasn't what was important right now; it didn't even register on her radar. She was Mari, manager of a four-star resort and she'd had to leave a lot of pain behind to get here. *Mariella* reminded her of things she kept trying to forget. How many times had her mother told her about her father's so-called family? The family she'd never known?

A family she never would know. Not now. It was just one of the missing gaps in her childhood.

"Mr. Fiori…" At his raised eyebrow she reluctantly amended, "Luca, I don't mean to sound impolite, but you are here as a representative of Fiori Resorts, here to evaluate your latest acquisition. My first name should be of little importance. Perhaps we should begin the tour now."

Luca took another bite of scone and considered how to answer. The general manager was a prickly sort, but pretty. And he did enjoy a challenge. "And miss out on this superior blend? I think not. We'll get to the rest. In time."

He sipped his coffee thoughtfully, letting his eyes roam over her. Her dark hair was pulled back into a simple, elegant twist, not a hair out of place. She had great legs, but she hid them beneath a conservative navy skirt and completed the look with an equally plain jacket. She gave new meaning to the words "power suit." Even her shoes…*dio mio*. His sister would have had a fit at the sight. Her shoes were plain, unadorned navy pumps. Hardly inspired. All in all she was a package that screamed "stay away."

Until she finally looked into his eyes, and then he knew.

Hers were stunning, nothing at all like the cold, efficient package she presented. They were gray-blue and smoky, soft and sexy, holding a lifetime of secrets.

"Mariella…" He let his voice soften and was

gratified to see her turn those eyes on him again. This was more than a challenge. This was unvarnished curiosity, something unusual for him. He was generally happy to skim the surface. On his arm was just about close enough for any woman to get. But there was something in Mari's eyes that drew him in. A mystery begging to be solved.

"Mari," she corrected coolly.

He frowned. Usually that soft tone worked on women. There was more to her than frosty order and sensible shoes, he could sense it. But as her eyes blazed at him, refusing to let him use her full name, he knew that this was one time his charm was going to fail him. With it came the unholy urge to laugh, along with grudging respect.

Who would have thought a trip to Canada would turn out to be so intriguing?

He had the most incredible desire to reach out and rest his fingers on her belligerent cheek. Even sitting on the stool, she was several inches below his face. So petite and feminine, even when she was standing her ground. What would she do if he tried such a thing? Blush? He didn't think so. Some of the women he knew would slap his face in a bout of indignant passion, but he didn't think Mari was the type for that, either.

No, an icy diatribe was more her style and he almost did it just to see what would happen. To see the sparks ignite, and flare.

Something held him back.

That wasn't why he was here. He was away from Italy, away from the constant demands and in a place where he alone could call the shots. He'd let himself be distracted before and it hadn't been pretty. It had cost him. Not quite so much as it had cost his father when his mother had walked out on them, but it had been adequately messy. He'd let Ellie make a fool of him. He'd risked his heart and had lost. No, his initial instinct was right. He would enjoy himself, but not take it any further than that.

He was here to make the Bow Valley Inn into the Fiori Cascade and in order to do that he had to *work* with Mariella Ross.

He stepped back. "Show me the rest, Mariella. And we'll see about taking the Fiori Cascade to a whole new level of opulence."

Luca stared at the papers once more, leaning back against the plush sofa and crossing his ankles on the coffee table. There was nothing really *wrong* with the hotel, not really. It was a nice establishment, comfortable, good service.

But *good* wasn't *Fiori*. His father had taught him that.

The new manager was something else, too. Mariella. Right now it appeared the only thing she shared with his grandmother was her name. She'd let down her guard for a few moments, but she was

a woman bound up in rules and boundaries, that much was crystal clear. All through the tour she'd mentioned how profitable or efficient their amenities were. Which was all well and good—he wanted to make a profit. But it wasn't the be all and end all. There was more to the Fiori brand than a balance sheet. It was what set Fiori apart from the rest.

He put the papers down and wandered over to his balcony. He slid open the door, crossing his arms against the chill of mountain fall air. Listening, he caught the whispered rustle of the wind through the gold-coin leaves of the trees below. He hadn't missed the way she kept putting distance between them, either. After that preliminary handshake, it had been like there was an invisible shield around her. The woman was a big contradiction. A sexy woman wrapped up in bubble-wrap. He wondered why.

And he really had to stop thinking about her.

He leaned against the railing, looking out over the white-capped range before him. He liked the gray stone exterior of the hotel, the way it mimicked the slate color of the peaks surrounding them. It reminded him of a small castle, a retreat tucked into the side of a mountain. A fortress.

A knock at the door shook him from his musings and he went back inside to answer it.

Mari had to struggle to keep her mouth from falling open when he opened the door. She completely

forgot about the file in her hand or her rea
going to the suite as soon as she saw him. Gone
the suit of earlier. Instead he wore jeans, old one.
The hem was slightly frayed, the thighs faded. And
he'd changed into a sweater, a ribbed tan pullover
that accentuated his lean build and complemented
his dark coloring. He looked completely ap-
proachable. Delicious.

This was ridiculous. She was staring at a vir-
tual stranger like he was a piece of the chef's
sachertorte. Good looks were just that. Good looks.
They said nothing about the man, nothing at all. A
man could hide behind his good looks. An all too
familiar ache spread through her chest.

"Mari. Come in."

He'd acquiesced and used the shortened version
of her name. She should have been grateful, but the
way he said it, the way the simple syllables rolled
off his tongue, sent flutters over her skin.

He reached out and took her hand and the skitters
fled, replaced by an automatic reaction. She pulled
her hand back, couching it along her side, and took
a step away from him.

His brows furrowed in the middle. Of course he
wouldn't understand.

Handshakes were a matter of business etiquette
and she tolerated it, but that was the extent of the
personal contact she could tolerate. Taking her hand
probably meant nothing to him. But to her it meant

taking a huge personal liberty. She couldn't help her reaction any more than she could change the past. She couldn't stop the fear, even when it was irrational as it was now. It didn't matter how much time went by, it was impossible to stop the instinctive reactions. He'd done nothing to make her believe he'd hurt her, but it didn't matter. The trigger was the same.

"I brought you the financial statements." She covered the uncomfortable moment by holding out the manila folder.

"You're serious?"

It was her turn to be confused, and she gratefully switched her focus to business. "Of course I am. I thought you'd need them."

"Are we in the black?"

"Of course we are!" When he didn't take the file, she lowered her arm again, hiding behind it.

"Then that's all I need to know."

"It is?"

"Please, sit down. Would you like a drink?"

"No, thank you."

She perched on the edge of an armchair like a bird waiting to take flight, while he walked over to the small bar. She noticed he was in his bare feet and for a moment her gaze was drawn to the frayed hem of his jeans, the way it rested against the skin of his heel.

She couldn't let his good looks distract her. She'd bet anything he was aware of his appearance and used it to his advantage all the time. But it wouldn't work with her. She wasn't so naive as that.

He wasn't interested in the numbers? Worry plunged through her stomach. What was he going to do to the hotel? Run it into the ground? Every decision she'd made in the last two and a half years had been carefully thought out, balanced against the pros and cons. What to do, where to live, what to wear and say… And he was treating this whole thing like it was no big deal. More and more he was bearing out her initial judgment. That for him this whole thing was a rich boy's game. But it was her livelihood. It was all she had. She'd built it from nothing. And he'd been given everything—life on a silver platter.

"What are your plans for the Cascade?" She spoke to his back as he poured a glass of red wine, filling a second glass despite her decline.

He returned and handed her the glass, then perched on the arm of the sofa. "I have many plans. I think revamping the hotel is going to be fun."

Fun? Her heart sank further. Great. He was charming, handsome. There was no denying it. In fact he was the first man she'd responded to physically ever since leaving Toronto. Her eyes narrowed. Acknowledging his good looks meant nothing except that she still had eyes to see with. Taking her livelihood in his hands for *fun* didn't sit well.

"Don't you think those sorts of decisions should be examined, weighed?"

"What's the fun in that?" His lips tipped up as he sipped his wine. "Aren't you going to have any? I brought it with me. It's Nico—the vineyards of my best friend, Dante Nicoletti. You'll like it—it's a fine Montepulciano. And it's a staple on all Fiori lists."

She dutifully sipped and looked down as the rich flavor surrounded her tongue. Oh, it was nice. Very nice. But that was hardly the point.

"I take my job seriously, Mr. Fiori. Not something to enjoy on a whim."

"Sometimes whims are the very best things." He smiled disarmingly and she found she actually had to work at not being charmed. Damn him!

She sipped again, sliding further back in the chair and crossing her legs. "I like what I do." Would she have called it fun? Probably not. But it gave her a sense of accomplishment. Working in a hotel in the majesty of the Rockies suited her wallflower qualities to a tee. She could glimpse the fairy tale while still being able to watch from the sidelines. She felt protected, and yet had room to breathe. But fun?

She wasn't sure she knew what fun was.

"But that's not the same thing. Tell me, Mari, what drives you? What makes you get up in the morning?"

The fact that I can.

She pushed the automatic answer away. She didn't have to justify her choices to him. He didn't need to know how she'd had a narrow escape, how it could have turned out so very differently years earlier.

"This isn't about me, it's about what's going to happen to this hotel. Paul Verbeek resigned when you bought the hotel. How much more is going to change? Staff is already upset at the possibility of change and insecurity. If I start handing out pink slips, morale's going to take a serious dip."

"That's the first thing you've said that I agree with."

She bristled. He waltzed in here and after what, four hours? decided she was wrong about just about everything. She knew how to do her job and she did it well, despite being new at it. This was going to be another case of owners sending in an emissary, turning everything upside down, then leaving the mess for local management to clean up. She sighed. Everything had been going fine. Why did this have to happen now?

"I don't know what to say. We obviously have differing opinions yet I have no wish to cause any discord. You're the boss." She folded her hands. One of them had to keep a logical head.

"Describe the Cascade in three words."

She squeezed her left fingers in her right hand. "Are you serious?"

"Perfectly. What are the first three words you think of when you think of this hotel?"

"Efficient. Class. Profitable." She shot the words out confidently. She prided herself—and the hotel—on them. It was the image she tried to portray every day.

He stopped pacing and sighed. "I was afraid of that."

"What's wrong with that? We have an efficient staff, an elegant establishment and we make a profit. You should be happy with all those things."

"Come here." He went to the balcony door again and slid it open. She followed, bringing the wine with her and cradling her glass in her hands. What on earth was he doing now?

"Look out over there."

The afternoon was waning and the sun's rays filtered through trees and shadows. Goose bumps rose on her skin at the chill in the air and she shivered.

"Just a minute," he murmured, disappearing back inside.

When he returned he draped a soft blanket over her shoulders and took the glass out of her hands. She tensed at his casual touch.

"Now look. And tell me, what do you see?"

"The valley, poplar trees, the river."

"No, Mari."

His body was close, too close and she fought against the panic rising instinctively in her chest. *Please don't touch me,* she prayed, torn between fear and an unfamiliar longing that he'd disobey her silent wishes. What would it feel like to have him cradle her body between his arms? Torture, or heaven? The way her heart was pounding, she recognized the sensation for what it was—fear.

As if he sensed her tension, he stepped to the side and gripped the iron railing. He breathed deeply, closed his eyes. When he opened them again he gazed over the vista before them.

"Freedom. Right now, what I'm feeling is freedom." His smile was wide and relaxed. "Look at this place. Look at where we are. There's no place in the world like *this* place. The Cascade can be a jewel in a beautiful kingdom. Wild and free on the outside. And inside…a place to rest, rejuvenate, to fall in love. Can't you feel it seducing you, Mari?"

Tears pricked her eyes but she blinked them away, gripping the edges of the blanket closely around her in a protective embrace.

Freedom. Rest. Rejuvenation. All the things she had spent years searching for, and exactly how she felt about her new life in this tiny resort town.

And with his good intentions, Luca Fiori was about to ruin it all.

CHAPTER TWO

"I DON'T understand."

Mari stepped back from the railing, away from the whispering trees and Luca's warm voice. He was talking castles and falling in love? She'd stopped believing in fairy tales a long time ago. "How exactly do you intend on accomplishing this?"

Before he could answer she scuttled back inside, removed the blanket from her shoulders and kept her hands busy by folding it. Having it around her shoulders had felt too much like an embrace and that didn't sit well. It was becoming increasingly clear that she and Luca were two very different people. She was firmly grounded in reality. Full stop.

He followed her, watching her from the glass door until she put the blanket down and then he stepped forward, giving her back the wine.

"I'm just working on impressions, for now."

"I prefer to work with facts, and so far all I've heard from you are nebulous statements of…of grandeur," she finished, faltering a little. Her heart pounded in her ears as she fought back the feeling that she was crossing an invisible line.

It was beginning to feel like an argument and she forced herself to relax, taking slow breaths and picturing the stress leaving through the soles of her feet. She hated conflict. With a passion. She'd learned to stick up for herself over the last few years but it didn't mean it came easily to her. If it weren't for the rest of the employees looking to her for leadership, she'd be tempted to back away and let him have a go at it rather than argue.

But she was the manager and if she wanted to keep that job, she needed to fight the battles that needed to be fought. People were depending on her. People who had been there for her since she'd made this her home, whether they knew it or not. She steeled her spine and made herself look up again.

"That's the problem with the Cascade," Luca explained. He poured a little more wine in his glass, took a sip and smiled a little. "Everything's been compartmentalized. One room says cool elegance and another is modern and another is rustic comfort…all admirable designs and styles, but without unity."

Unity?

His hand spread wide. "We need to decide what the Cascade is. What it means…what we want to achieve…and then work around that. If we work on one area at a time, it means less disturbance to everyone. The goal is to make everything exemplify Fiori Cascade."

Mari's eyes widened. "That will cost a fortune."

"Fiori has deep pockets."

"Of course…I'm just…weighing the cost versus the benefit. The Bow Val…I mean the Cascade is already doing well. Look at the numbers—we have excellent capacity even for this time of year."

"That's not remotely the point."

And there was where they differed. She realized that they did not see *anything* the same way. Maybe it was having money and security that made the difference. Luca didn't have to worry where his next meal was coming from, or where he'd sleep, or what the future held because his was there waiting for him. It always had been. But her life wasn't that way. It was planning and dollars and cents and making the most out of less, rocking the boat as little as possible. It was staying in the background, out of notice, causing little trouble. And there was nothing wrong with that. It had gotten her where she was. She worked quietly but effectively and she'd been rewarded for it through steady promotion.

"If you implement all these great ideas, when can we expect the memo from head office telling us to downsize our staff?"

"That won't happen."

"Will you guarantee that in writing? Because I've seen it happen, the expenditures are too great to sustain staffing and layoffs occur. Are you planning on closing us down during renovations? What are these people to do then? They count on their pay to put food on the table. Have you considered that?"

A smile flickered on Luca's face and Mari steeled herself against the onslaught of charm she knew was coming. This was important. As much as she wanted to back away and say, "Yes sir, whatever you want sir," she wouldn't.

"Of course I'm not shutting the hotel down, don't be ridiculous. And if any employees aren't required during refurbishing, they'll get paid vacation. Will that suit you?"

"I want it in writing," Mari reiterated, and put down her wineglass. He was the boss, and she was treading perilously close to insubordination. She thought back to the timid girl who had started working here only a few years ago. It was the people in this very hotel that had helped her. She wouldn't let them down now.

"You are a sharp one." His voice held a touch of irritation and she felt the warm thread of slight victory infuse her. She'd gotten to him, then. His implacable charm was faltering and it emboldened her.

"I'm no one's yes-man."

"I'm beginning to see that." His gaze appraised her and she felt a flush climb her cheeks. It felt as though the air in her chest expanded. No, no, no. She had to keep focused on work!

"Perhaps tomorrow we might schedule a meeting to go over the preliminary details."

"I have a better idea."

Mari met his eyes yet again, and for a moment the air seemed to hum between them. The annoyance of moments ago was dispelled as he slid one hand into his jeans pocket. His eyes were warm, crinkled at the corners as he smiled at her.

"Have dinner with me tonight."

She took two steps back as sure footing flew out the window. Alarm bells started ringing in her head. "Absolutely not."

"Here, in the hotel. It'll be a business supper. What is it you say…scout's honor? Strictly work." He lifted a finger to his forehead.

"It's two fingers, and dinner is hardly a business meeting."

Luca stepped forward, putting his glass down on a side table with a small click that echoed in the silence.

He was too close again. Part of her held the thread of panic and the other part was drawn to him, plain and simple, which meant that nothing was simple at *all*. It was much easier when they were disagreeing. Easier to keep him at a distance. She wasn't equipped to deal with his charm. He didn't even seem to know he possessed it.

"Bring your day planner if that makes you happy." Happy? Huh. He was flirting, and she didn't flirt. Ever!

"I think my office tomorrow would be much better."

"Yes, but you see I need to get a complete picture, and that includes the quality of the dining experience. And eating alone does not constitute a fine dining experience, in my opinion."

Oh, he was good. Smooth and persuasive and actually logical! She couldn't find a good argument. How could she tell him why she didn't go out to dinner with anyone? How she went home each night and made a meal for one and ate it with Tommy, her dog? Flimsy at best. And the real reason was none of his business. Not his, not anyone's. No one here knew how she'd run away. How she still looked over her shoulder.

"A working dinner."

"Of course."

There was no polite way out of it. He was here, all the way from Italy, he was her boss and he was calling the shots. Like it or not. She'd pushed him as far as she'd dared just now and her victory was thin. If they were to work together for the next several weeks, months even…her heart quivered at the thought… then somehow they needed to reach an amicable status quo. She swallowed. He had to know she was not afraid. He had to know she put the hotel and its employees first.

"One dinner, that's all. And we discuss work."

"Naturally."

Mari took a few sidesteps, thankful the door

was within reach. "I'll meet you in the Panorama Room at six."

"Perfect."

When he walked toward her she pulled open the door, a little too quickly to be poised. His hand gripped the door frame above her shoulder and she felt the heat from his body. Too close. She wasn't sure if the tripping of her pulse was fear or exhilaration. She slid out the opening as fast as she possibly could, clinging to whatever grace she could muster.

"I'll see you then," Luca said softly.

She fled for the elevator without looking back.

It was 5:57 when Mari stopped before the entrance of the dining room and smoothed her dress.

She paused in the door, scanning the room, but he wasn't there. Relief warred with annoyance. She didn't have to worry about making an entrance this way, but at least he could be on time. She wanted to get this over with. It was irritating to have her initial impressions of him confirmed so accurately. Luca was unfocused, cavalier about the whole thing. He was every bit the playboy she'd read about. Sexy and smooth. Working together was going to drive her crazy.

She was shown to the best table in the room. She took her seat with surprise, looked outside at the mountains and trees being thrown into shadow by twilight. She hadn't asked for this particular table;

it was one usually reserved for guests requesting something "special." It would be very wrong of them to monopolize the table when there was likely a paying guest waiting for it.

She sipped her drink and waited. By ten past six her toes had joined her nails, tapping with impatience. Only to stop abruptly when he stepped in the room.

God, he was beautiful. She could admit it when he was a room away from her and they weren't embroiled in business. He was safe there. Safe and devastatingly sexy in black trousers and a white shirt. She shook her head, sighing. It was one of those tailored shirts that was meant to be untucked, emphasizing his narrow waist and moving up to broad shoulders. One hand slid casually into his pocket in a gesture she somehow already knew intimately. He said something to the hostess at the front, and the two of them laughed.

Luca Fiori was every woman's dream. Everyone's but hers. Dreams like that simply didn't last. But it didn't mean she couldn't appreciate the package. It *was* a lovely package. And for a very quick moment, she wished. Wishing wasn't a luxury she afforded herself. But looking at Luca, with his bronzed skin and easy smile, she wished she knew how to be that free. To be able to accept, and to give.

He approached the table with an easy stride. "I'm sorry I'm late. I got caught up in e-mails my father sent and lost track of time."

She pursed her lips, determined not to let him off

easily, but he leaned over and pressed an informal kiss of greeting to her cheek.

She froze.

Seemingly unaware of her reaction, Luca took the chair across from her. "You look beautiful. Have you ordered?"

Beautiful? Her? She'd gone home to change and feed Tommy and then he'd drooled over the front of her outfit, causing a wardrobe change. Gone was the tailored charcoal trouser suit she'd picked and in its place was her generic little black dress—simply cut, black velvet with long fitted sleeves and with a hem ending just above the knee.

It wasn't as businesslike as she'd have preferred, but it worked and while classy there wasn't much sexy about it. It seemed compliments rolled off his tongue as easily as assurances.

"Thank you, and no, I was enjoying a drink and the music." Mari struggled to make her voice sound less strangled than she felt.

A recent jazz CD played over the speakers. She hadn't paid it a whit of attention but needed to cover. It was becoming clear that Luca was a toucher. He was comfortable with easy, physical gestures like polite kisses and hand clasps. It should help, knowing they were impersonal, but Mari knew she could never be that tactile with people. It was simply too difficult. Yet to explain was unthinkable. She'd just have to muddle through.

"I ordered us some wine on the way in. I'm looking forward to tasting something more local."

Brenda came back with a bottle and moved to uncork it, but Luca took it from her hands. "Thank you, Brenda, but I can do this."

Mari looked at him, tilting her head as he applied the corkscrew to the bottle. He was new, and likely jet-lagged, but he'd remembered Brenda's name. She couldn't help but be impressed. It showed an attention to detail that surprised her, and people didn't often surprise her.

He pulled out the cork with a minimum of fuss and put the bottle down briefly. "You haven't said anything."

"I'm waiting to get to the business portion of the meal."

She set her lips and looked him dead in the eye. A deal was a deal. As long as he kept it about the Cascade they'd have no problems.

He chuckled as he poured wine into two glasses. "Single-minded. I like that. It means you're focused, driven."

"A compliment."

"Perhaps. I'm reserving judgment. Waiting to see if you're also rigid, stubborn and always need to be right."

Mari grabbed her tonic water as her face flamed. Of all the nerve!

"I don't apologize for being organized or efficient."

"Nor should you. They're admirable qualities."

Mari looked out the window and away from him. She'd never met a man like him. She couldn't quite pin him down and that threw her off balance. Normally she could typecast a person within moments of meeting. She put them in a file in her mind and dealt with them accordingly.

But not Luca. There was something different about him that she couldn't put her finger on. He was very urban with his carefully messed hair, the way he left his collar open so that Mari was treated to a tempting glimpse of the tanned hollow of his throat. As he lifted his glass she spied a ring on his right hand…plain, not ostentatious at all. It almost looked antique. In the centre of the flat gold oval was the imprint of a lily. The same imprint that she recognized from the company logo. It was the only jewelry he wore. His entire demeanor suggested playboy, but there was something more.

"Let's order," he suggested, his voice drawing her eyes away from the ring. "We'll talk about the food and brainstorm about what the Cascade will become."

He flipped open his menu, skimmed it and shut it again.

"Just like that?"

"Absolutely."

Mari looked down at her own menu, though she could recite it without seeing the words. Everything about him threw her off her stride. Just when she credited him with not making decisions, he surprised her by being annoyingly definitive.

"We should switch tables. There's usually a wait for this one and our guests do come first."

Luca regarded her over his glass. "No need. I took care of it."

"And how, may I ask, did you do that?"

His smile was disarming. She noticed again the sensual curve of his lips and wondered what cruel joke the universe was playing, sending such a man for her to deal with. She was completely out of her depth and drowning fast.

"I called the room, spoke to a lovely gentleman who is here celebrating his twentieth anniversary with his wife. I explained who I was and said that the hotel would be happy to treat him—and his wife—to a five-course meal in their room, along with a bottle of champagne."

Mari's lips dropped open before she could help it. Mentally she added up the cost of such a thing. It was selfish. Indulgent. All so he could have the best table.

"It would have been easier, and cheaper, for us to simply eat at a different table."

Luca ran a finger down the leather spine of the menu, a smile playing on his lips. "Perhaps. But they get an anniversary to remember and I get to enjoy the sight of you at the best table in the house. It is…how do you put it? A no-brainer."

She ignored the compliment. "It's self-indulgent."

"Of course. Shouldn't the Cascade be about indulgence?"

She lowered her voice to a whisper that hissed across the table. "You're going to indulge us right out of business!"

A waiter came to take their order. Without missing a beat, Luca ordered the Harvest Squash Soup and Pancetta Salmon, while she scanned the menu once more. In the heat of the discussion, she'd forgotten what she wanted, and the gap of silence was awkward.

"The pasta, Ms. Ross?" the waiter suggested. She closed the leather cover and nodded. When the menus were taken away, Luca leaned forward, close enough she could smell the light, masculine scent of his cologne. Exclusive, expensive and somehow perfectly Luca. Her pupils widened as he took the finger that had caressed the menu and ran it lightly over her wrist. The action surprised her so much she couldn't even think to pull away.

"Mr. and Mrs. Townsend will have an incomparable anniversary night. Mr. Townsend is a prominent attorney, did you know that? His wife is involved in several charities. What do you think they'll say to their friends when they return home? That the room was lovely? That the mountains were splendid? That could be said of nearly every hotel in this area." He withdrew his finger from the delicate skin of her wrist and looked in her eyes. "They will remark at how special they felt. The delightful meal served in their room by attentive staff. The complimentary champagne and the single red rose presented to Mrs. Townsend."

He sat back, satisfied. "Don't underestimate the power of a happy customer, Mari. We'll more than earn back what dinner cost. The Townsends will come back. And they'll likely bring a trail of friends and associates with them. They'll remember the romance."

His eyebrows lifted as it dawned. "That's it. That's what the Cascade needs to become. Get out your day planner, Mari."

He changed tack so often she was having difficulty following. "What on earth are you talking about?"

"The Fiori Cascade. Remember the Romance." He clapped his hands together then reached for his wine. "This room—the Panorama. It's romantic, don't you think?" He didn't wait for her answer. "Look at the color, the furnishings. Timeless, nostalgic, reminiscent of a golden age. Gleaming wood, rich scarlet and gold. A place where women feel beautiful and wooed. A place to slow down, be indulged, pampered. Chandeliers and fine wine and…"

He paused.

"You're not saying anything."

"I can't get a word in edgewise." Mari left her

planner right where it was. By tomorrow his ideas could have changed a half dozen times, for all she knew.

"You don't like it? You don't agree?"

"I think you're getting carried away with an idea."

"Oh, but, Mari ideas are the best part." He reached out and clasped her hand. "There is nothing more exciting than looking and seeing all the possibilities."

She pulled her hand away, cradling it in her lap. Luca carried on as if he hadn't noticed her abrupt withdrawal. "Taking a vision and making it reality is the best part of my job."

Their first course was served. Mari watched as Luca tried the soup, closed his eyes and murmured, "Mmm."

She stared at the full curve of his lips, shocked to feel the stirrings of attraction in the midst of such animosity. Instantly those stirrings were followed by numbing fear. It wouldn't matter. She wasn't capable of relationships. She was done with trusting and taking risks. That she'd suddenly gone from physical appreciation to attraction startled her sufficiently to keep her on task. She stabbed at her greens like she was wielding a pitchfork.

He looked around and Mari tried to see what he was seeing. People enjoying fine food in an elegant setting. It's what they paid for, what they expected.

How would the rest of the hotel look, if it followed in the tradition of this room?

"What are you thinking?" He put down his spoon and she felt his eyes on her.

"Just wondering." The trouble was, she *could* see it. Could see how stunning, marvelous it would be. Like stepping back in time.

"Trust me, Mari."

She dropped her eyes and focused on spearing a large chunk of walnut from her salad. "I can't."

"Don't you feel the beauty here? This room...this is what the Cascade should embody. It's warm, it's cozy, yet it's rich and opulent at the same time. From the outside it's a castle. On the inside...it needs to be an embrace. When guests are here they need to be soaked in beauty."

"Please." That one word was ripe with disdain. She could not be wooed by pretty words, and he'd been doling out more than his share. Pretty words did not keep a four-star hotel profitable. Pretty words did not...would not keep her in line.

"You're worried about the money. And details."

"Bingo."

Luca picked up his spoon again, ate some soup. "I'll tell you what, Mari. I'll start making some notes. I'll even put some preliminary figures together...just for you."

"You're too kind." She didn't attempt to disguise the sarcasm. It was becoming increasingly clear that

Luca was full of grand schemes and she was going to have her hands full keeping him out of the clouds and on the ground.

"Mari?"

She raised her eyebrows.

"Why are you so determined to dislike me?"

She looked away from the steady gaze. There was nothing condemning in it, just a curiosity that burned through her.

It wasn't that she didn't want to like him or dislike him. It was more a matter of self-preservation. She didn't like change, didn't work well with change. And it was everything Luca represented. She'd worked so hard to get where she was, to feel comfortable and established and…safe. And he waltzed in, in his expensive clothes and sexy smile and wanted to change everything. And with a method that made no sense to her. All of a sudden *safe* wasn't a sure thing.

"It's not about liking or disliking, Luca. It's about the changes. You're changing more than the name. You're changing things that some of us have worked very hard to maintain. I've put a lot of time and energy into this hotel and perhaps I feel like that's being swept away without a moment's consideration. Meanwhile all of us here will remain long after you're gone. When you're done, you can wash your hands of it. We're left to deal with what comes after." He'd blow through like a whirlwind, and what destruction would be left in his wake?

Luca leaned forward, linking his hands on the white cloth on the table. "I understand that, really I do. But this is where you have to trust me. This is what I do, Mari. This is what my family has done for decades. I know my job and I'm good at it. If I weren't, Fiori wouldn't be nearly as successful as it is. I'm not going to throw you…or the staff…out along with the old carpet. I promise."

And oh, she wanted to believe him. Desperately. But trust was a very rare commodity.

"You also need to consider how this will affect us financially. The reality of it. It cannot be ignored." *I can't be ignored,* she thought, but swallowed it away. This wasn't about her, not really.

"Reality is overrated. What we're selling is an experience, an escape, a fantasy."

He leaned over so that the enticing scent of his cologne tickled her nose once more. His toffee-eyes captured hers. "When was the last time you indulged in a fantasy, Mari?"

CHAPTER THREE

MARI stopped, smoothed her skirt first and then her hair, before knocking on the door that used to be to her office before she became general manager.

"Come in."

It was odd, finding her new boss sitting in her old chair, but she pushed the feeling aside. He needed a working area and she was now in the general manager's office. It didn't make sense to feel he was taking over her space. She was the one with the big office now.

She'd had to push a lot of feelings aside this morning, like the lingering fear that flickered in her belly when she remembered her dream of last night. There was no sense worrying about the fact that the dream was back. She would just chalk it up to the chocolate she'd indulged in last night at dessert. That, paired to the chaos that was rapidly becoming her life, explained it away. Even if she couldn't quite shake the darkness of it from her system. Considering the letter she'd received two days ago, it wasn't surprising. She hated the thought of Robert being up for parole. Hated the way the mere mention of his name paralyzed her. Focusing on work was the only thing keeping her sane. And Luca wasn't making it any easier. He'd featured in her dream as well. But she had to shake it and be objective.

This was about today, about figuring out what it was Luca planned to do and exerting some of her own caution over the procedure. He would do whatever he wanted. She'd realized that after their dinner last night. But she was no pushover. Not anymore. She would keep things logical, reasonable. Within boundaries. In *all* ways.

"Mari! Good morning." He gave a click of the mouse before pushing back his chair. "I was just sending an e-mail to my sister in Florence. Sharing my ideas and getting her input. She's got a fantastic eye."

"Then why didn't *she* come?" The question was out before Mari could think and her cheeks bloomed at her rudeness.

"Because she has a three-year-old and a baby to look after. I'm hoping she'll make it out next summer, when the refurbishing is complete and the landscaping done. As it is, she's nagging me to be back home for Christmas."

"You think we'll be done that soon?"

"Shoulder season is the best time to renovate. I can always come back after the holiday and finish things off."

Mari stood awkwardly in the doorway, unsure of how to proceed. Her blazer pocket contained half a dozen messages she should answer and she knew there were matters that needed her attention on her desk. So why didn't she get to it?

"Did you need something in particular?" Luca posed the question, raising his eyebrows and Mari felt even more awkward.

"No, not really. I'll just, um, go to my office, and if you need me for anything you can find me there."

"I'm waiting for a call from a designer. He did some work for us when we bought the Colorado Springs property and with the similarity in settings, I thought bringing him up here would be a good idea. I know what I want, but I'm at a loss when it comes to deciding fabrics and tapestries and…well, it's Dean's job to take my vision and put it all together."

Her mouth went dry. Nine o'clock in the morning and he was already moving forward without even discussing things with her. Was this all going to happen without her, then? "And what's my job in all this?"

For a moment she was afraid he was going to get up and her fingers felt for the handle of the door. Briefly she remembered the touch of his finger on her wrist last night. But he merely crossed an ankle over his knee and smiled up at her. "Your job is to keep the hotel running as seamlessly as possible for our guests and staff. I can already see you're good at it. And your job is also to help me. I do want your input, Mari."

When the phone on his desk rang, his attention slid away from her completely, and she felt like a child dismissed from the principal's office. Damn, she'd come in here hoping to get some insight into his plans, figure out a way to retain at least some control over the whole business. And she was leaving with nothing.

Mari made her way to the manager's office in a daze. It was clear she wasn't needed when it came to whatever changes were impending. As far as Luca was concerned, she was there to keep people happy.

She shut her office door firmly and threw her purse on her chair. She hadn't worked this hard to build up her life to have someone dismiss it like it didn't matter. Her years of being a doormat were over. She thought of the court proceedings happening this very moment and lifted her chin. She smoothed her hands over her cheeks, trying to soothe away the nagging feeling of inadequacy. She wouldn't let him do this to her. This was *her* life now, and she would hold on to it with both hands.

He was bringing in a designer, of course he was. That was logical. But it was all happening so quickly. She wanted everything back the way it was.

Luca would consult with this designer and she'd be out of the decision-making process. She couldn't let that happen. If she did he'd start making unilateral decisions that affected everyone. He'd have all the control and the thought terrified her.

But how could she hold her ground, when the very thought of asserting herself into the situation made her stomach tremble and her knees watery?

She had to come up with something that showed her value. When the idea hit she was shocked she hadn't thought of it before. The hotel had an attic. And with every renovation, she knew certain things had been placed there for storage. She was sure there was a trove of antiques from the original design up there. She remembered what he'd said last night about returning to a "golden age." Rich fabrics and natural wood. If she remembered correctly, there was an old chandelier, and who knew what other treasures she'd find?

She jumped up from her chair, ignoring the open file on her desk and grabbing instead a ring of keys from the back of her desk drawer. She was just turning into the hall when she ran smack-dab into the solid wall of his chest.

"Allentare!" He gripped her arms to steady her and she stiffened beneath his fingers. "Mari, slow down! Are you all right?"

"Let me go. I'm fine." She shook off his hands and straightened her shoulders.

The woman was as prickly as a cactus. Luca stood back, nonplussed. She'd nearly knocked him over and now stood glaring at him like it was his fault that she'd come storming out of her office, not looking where she was going.

"I am glad to hear it."

Her face softened just a bit. "I beg your pardon, it was my fault."

"It doesn't matter. I was just coming to see you."

He watched as she slowly relaxed. First a deep breath, then her shoulders lowered and the taut lines of her face disappeared. She was wound as tight as a top. She had been last night, too. Her cheek had been cold when he'd kissed it in greeting and the tiny touch on her wrist seemed to turn her to stone. The woman needed to deflate before she imploded.

She placed a polite smile on her lips, one he knew was put there for show and not genuine. It was a cover. But what was she covering? He'd never met a woman so uptight and rigid. He had a feeling if he said black, she'd say white just to be contrary. In that way, he thought ruefully, she wasn't that different from his father. He held back the sigh gathering in his lungs. The Cascade was his baby. He'd demanded full authority over everything. And when it was over he'd be able to take the credit and finally step out within the company in his own right. He loved his father, he did. It didn't mean he wanted to work under his thumb for the rest of his life. It was the one thing that kept things tense between them.

"Did you need something?"

At the sound of her voice he dragged his gaze from her lips. "Need? I heard back from the designer, Dean Shiffling." He couldn't keep the annoyance out of his voice. "He can't make it until day after tomorrow. I told him we'd send a car to meet him at the airport."

They'd taken half a dozen steps down the hall but she halted abruptly. "Luca, we don't have a car. We have a shuttle van."

"Fiori does not herd guests into a, what did you call it? A shuttle van." He muttered something under his breath. There was much to be said for the old Inn, but things needed to change to bring it up to Fiori standards. "I shall look after getting us proper transportation."

He started walking again, knowing she'd have no choice but to follow after him. Already he could see the adding machine whirring in her head, working sums. A smile played with the corners of his lips. Perhaps it was wrong, but he had to admit he enjoyed putting her off balance. It had been too long since he'd had a worthy opponent to butt heads with and he got the feeling that Mari would be up to the challenge. It was worth it to see that firelight in her gray-blue eyes and her color rise. So much better than her icy withdrawal.

They stepped into the lobby area. "What did you want to see me about?" he asked, surveying the lobby. He looked at the floor. They'd get rid of some of those fussy carpets, polish the stone beneath. And the lighting was wrong. This lobby was comfortable but cluttered. It needed space, and light amongst the richness. Let them play off each other.

"I didn't. You ran into me, remember?"

"Ah, yes. A happy accident indeed." He let his eyes twinkle at her. "And you were in a spectacular rush."

"I thought of something this morning that may come in handy during your redecorating."

"Yes?" She had his attention.

"And you're noticeably agitated that your designer isn't at your beck and call within the hour."

His eyebrow raised at that. She was going to keep him on his toes. She was correct. He'd wanted to get started right away and he was being forced to wait.

"Perhaps."

"And people always do what you tell them."

"Usually, yes. With a notable exception." He aimed a pointed glare at her.

She held up a key.

She was playing with him now and it amused him as much as annoyed him. She'd never once in their meetings shown a fun side. "I'm assuming that is to a door. A door you're going to tell me about."

The faintest of smiles cracked her face. She looked very different when she put away that cold façade. Her eyes lightened and she seemed almost like a precocious child. Like there was more to her than fusty suits that covered as much skin as possible and prim hairstyles. He stared at the utilitarian twist and wondered what it would look like if she let it down. If it would be soft and pliant. Like her skin. He remembered the feel of the nearly translucent skin just beneath her palm. Would the rest of her be as fragile and soft?

Now that wouldn't be wise at all. Even if a man couldn't help but wonder.

"I was going to check it out first, but I suppose you want to come along. It's to the attic."

"You've an attic?"

Her smile grew as she nodded. "We do. And if we find what I think is there, you're going to be happy I thought of it. Then you can stop obsessing about getting your designer in and focus on something else."

He ignored the barb, too excited by the idea of a treasure hunt. "Then lead on, by all means."

They took the service elevator to the top floor. Stepping out into a windowless corridor, Mari stepped to the right toward a large double door. "This is our storage area. I remembered it this morning. Something you said last night twigged with me, about a golden age." She turned the key in the lock and pushed the door open.

Inside was like finding buried treasure. A film of dust covered everything: chairs, tables, desks, divans, even paintings and sculptures. A room full of potential, waiting to be rediscovered. The hotel must have been a glory in its early days, Luca thought, before someone came along and decided to change it. His eyes lit on a particularly fine tallboy.

Whoever had relegated it to the attic should have been whipped. It was too fine, too valuable, to be hidden away in an airless, forgotten room.

"Dear God." Luca stepped inside. There was little order to it, but he knew already she'd uncovered a gold mine. Excitement drummed in his veins. He wasn't changing the hotel at all. He was restoring it. The idea thrilled him. He enjoyed the creating part of his job so much more than the management. It was a large reason why he wanted to step out of his father's shadow. "Why are these things not displayed?"

"I can only assume that renovations over the years have relegated them to the bench."

"The bench?"

"You know, when sports players aren't on the field. They're benched."

"Right." He stepped around an old rolltop desk, a layer of dust hiding what he knew would be a gleaming walnut finish. "Feel it, Mari. There's history in this room. So much history." If only Dean could be here sooner. They'd take an inventory and choose which pieces would be used in the decoration. Luca wanted to start right now.

But perhaps now was the time to explore.

He looked over at Mari. Prickly as thorns, but he could tell she was enjoying this. It was in the way her eyes lit up, or her fingers daintily touched the back of a tufted chair. She was picking her way to the far right, stepping gingerly and careful not to disturb the dust. She was a careful one, he was coming to understand. Always a deliberate move. Always a purpose. He wondered why. What had made her so cautious, when it was clear that inside she had vision fighting to get out?

"Here it is."

He gave a plush wine velvet divan a longing look as he passed by, making his way to her. Only to find her standing beside a huge gilt and crystal chandelier that had been hidden by two armoires.

"It's seen better days. But I thought I remembered it here."

Luca reached out and touched a large teardrop shaped crystal, sending it tinkling against identical drops. "It's stunning. It's perfect."

"It *is* lovely."

Luca looked up at her. Ah, so the chandelier's magic wasn't all lost on her. The wistful turn of her lips told him so. A tendril of hair had come loose from her ever-present bun and kissed her cheek. She looked up at him and their eyes met, held. He could already picture the chandelier gracing the ballroom, the shots of light glancing off the crystals on to the gleaming floor and polished wood. Could picture Mari in the middle of it, slim and elegant in a golden evening dress, smiling at him. She was, he realized, cool class and grace. Timeless. His ingénue.

"You love it, too. I can see it on your face."

Something changed at his words, breaking the spell. Her eyes cooled and she straightened her shoulders, looking away. "It makes perfect sense to use these things if they fit in with your renovations. Much cheaper than purchasing new."

"Oh, it's not about the money, don't pretend otherwise. Look at this place." He turned, laughing to himself to shake away the intensity he'd felt in the moment. At least she was consistent, protesting about the bottom line. But he'd seen the look of longing in her eyes and he'd wanted her to look at him that way. Every moment she intrigued him more, but he was also increasingly aware that she wasn't the kind of woman a man trifled with. He forced himself back to the task. "Each of these pieces has a story, can't you feel it?"

He took a few steps and stopped in front of a gilded mirror. He swiped a hand over the glass, clearing a stripe of dust away. "Oh, Mari, such beautiful pieces. Neglected for so long, forgotten. Just waiting for someone to discover them and make them new again. To make them shine."

When she said nothing, he looked back. She was trapped with the armoires on one side, the chandelier on the other and he was blocking her path back to the door. She was standing so very still, as if he'd struck her, and he didn't know why. He got the sense that she was crying, but that was ridiculous because her eyes were bone-dry in her pale face. For some odd reason he wanted to erase the distance between them and take her in his arms. As soon as he thought it, he mentally stepped backward.

Enjoying playing cat and mouse was one thing. Having fanciful thoughts was well and good. Acting on it was another. And this situation was already complicated enough without him adding to it by getting involved with the hotel manager. It wouldn't be suitable. It would be messy. And he didn't do messy relationships. He didn't do *any* relationships at all, beyond the no-strings-attached ones. He'd determined long ago not to let his heart get involved with a woman. He never wanted to give a woman the power to destroy him the way his mother had his father. The way Ellie had nearly destroyed him.

"Please excuse me, I need to get back. If you'll lock the door when you leave…"

She took halting steps toward him, cueing him to move out of the way. But he couldn't, not hearing that cold, dry tone in her voice. He didn't know what he'd said to cause such a reaction but he knew for certain that she was not all right and that superceded his own concerns.

She stopped a few feet from him. "Please, excuse me," she repeated, her eyes gray against her washed-out pallor.

He started to step aside so she could pass, but at the last moment he couldn't let her go without checking she was okay. He moved forward, reached out, clasped her elbow.

"Get your hands off me."

She said it quietly, calmly, but the underlying venom in it shocked him so much that he stepped back, immediately releasing her elbow. He hadn't thought it possible but she paled even further.

"Don't ever touch me again," she said stridently, as she quickly picked a path around the scattered forgotten furniture. She scrambled out the door, leaving it open. Seconds later he heard the elevator pause, open and close again.

He sat down on the nearest chair, releasing a puff of dust. He'd only been trying to be a gentleman when she was clearly in distress. It was obvious that whatever attraction he'd felt earlier was not reciprocated. She was cold, irritating, dictatorial. Nothing but a complication. He should fire her and get on with turning the Fiori Cascade into the hotel it was meant to be.

But he couldn't do that. She was good at what she did, he could tell. He'd promised her no one would lose their jobs. That had included her.

And Luca Fiori was a man of his word.

When he went back to the administration offices, her door was closed. He knocked, then opened it.

It was like the scene upstairs had never happened. Her suit was straight, brushed of any dust. Her color was back, enhanced by fresh lipstick and her hair was tidied, even more severely pinned in place, if that were possible.

The sting of the insult had worn away and he'd been left with the very empty knowledge that for some unknown reason, Mari was afraid of him.

"I wanted to make sure you were all right."

She looked up from what she was writing and pasted on what he was rapidly coming to understand was her face-the-public smile. "I'm fine, thank you. A little behind after our tour, though." She looked back down at her paper and began writing again.

He wrinkled his brow. The woman before him was cool, assured, in control. A direct contrast to the woman who'd nearly come unglued the moment he'd put a hand on her elbow. A woman practiced at hiding her feelings, who happened to have slipped and let him witness a weak moment.

He should nod and walk away. It was none of his business. But then he remembered the stark look of nakedness he'd seen on her face when he'd spoken of the antiques. She'd looked like a woman who'd been stripped bare. He couldn't ignore that, even if he wanted to. If he let this go now, it would stand between them the entire time they worked together. It would be far better to get it out in the open. Move on.

"Do you want to talk about it, Mari?"

With a sigh she put down the pen, placed her

hands flat on her desk and crossed her legs. "Talk about what, Luca?"

"About what happened in the attic."

She looked away. "No, I don't."

"You were frightened. I want to know why."

"I was not frightened. I happen to be…claustro-phobic."

It was paltry and he saw through it. But he could not make her talk and he hardly knew her well enough to pry. Still…

"I did not realize that when I reached for your arm."

Her hands remained flat on the blotter and she met his eyes coolly. "Luca, I am a person who does not like her personal space invaded. I'm not a touchy person. That's all. I'm sorry if that is blunt, or rude."

"It is honest, and I appreciate it. So it is not just me you don't want to touch you, it is everyone."

Her cheeks flamed. "That's correct."

"It's nothing personal."

She swallowed, and his gaze was drawn to the curve of her throat. Damn, it sure felt personal right now.

"Nothing personal," she echoed weakly.

"I'm glad, because we will be working together closely and it will be difficult if there is animosity between us."

Animosity?

Mari swallowed and forced the cool, neutral expression to remain on her face. He had no idea about what had happened in the attic. How his words touched her, mirrored so many of her own emotions. How she'd suddenly felt strangled and had to get out.

He'd touched her.

She hated being touched. And when he'd gripped her elbow, something had shot through her that terrified her.

But it wasn't memory. It was longing. Something she hadn't felt for so long the very presence of it undid her. She *liked* the feel of his hand on her elbow, connecting them. Liked it so much she'd wanted to slide forward into his arms and let them surround her. Protect her.

She'd vowed no man would touch her ever again, and until now she'd never wanted one to. Oh, nothing made sense! She'd had to escape, pull herself together.

She risked a look up. He was watching her steadily and she knew there was something *very* personal between them, like it or not. Something she refused to acknowledge further than she already had. She wasn't equipped for more than accepting there was a small level of attraction. Anything more would be pointless.

"I assure you, it has nothing to do with you." And the bottom line was, it didn't. It had to do with her and with Robert and that was all.

"Then I won't take it personally. I merely wanted to be sure you were all right."

"I am, and thank you for asking."

When she smiled this time it was without the frosty veneer. He had accepted what she'd said with politeness and grace. She was touched that someone cared enough to be concerned about her. No one worried about her, because she'd reinvented her life that way. But without even knowing her, Luca seemed to care. It was unexpected, and though she suspected he'd hate the thought, it was sweet.

He stepped forward and laid the key on her desk. "I thought you might want this back."

She left it where he'd placed it and he stepped away.

He was nearly to the door when he turned back. "Oh, and Mari, I'd like for you to sit in on the meeting with Dean once I've given him the tour and my initial ideas. We'll work up a preliminary budget and tentative schedule, get the ball rolling so to speak, and that's your forte. I also would like us to send out a joint memo before then to all the staff. Something to say that over the next months there will be changes and adjustments, but that no one will lose their position. That every effort will be made to make this as seamless as possible for both staff and guests. I keep my promises, Mari. I hope you remember that."

He was keeping his word. It pleased her that he remembered. When she least expected it, he showed consideration to those around him. Perhaps he was more than she'd initially suspected.

Perhaps the playboy from the glossy magazines had a little more substance than she'd given him credit for.

"I'll draft one up today and e-mail it to you."

"Thank you, Mari."

She got up from her desk finally, knowing that she owed him something, even if she didn't know what. She picked up the key and held it out. When he reached with his hand, she pressed the key into his palm.

"Keep it. I have another somewhere."

His fingers closed over hers slightly as he cupped the key in his hand. She tried very hard to ignore the tingles shivering up her arm at the warmth of his fingers.

"You're sure?"

Mari remembered his face as he'd walked into the attic. She'd put up walls because she'd resented the easy joy he'd had, seeing the dusty antiques. She didn't let herself feel things like that anymore. It would be petty to deprive him of it. It was his hotel, and he was keeping his end of the bargain.

"I'm sure, Luca. And when Mr. Shiffling arrives, we'll meet and discuss how best to approach the changes to come."

"Then I'll hear from you later today."

He pulled his hand from hers and pocketed the key. He walked back to his office, and moments later she heard the door click. But she stood in the middle of her own, wondering how on earth she was going to handle the roller coaster that was rapidly becoming her life.

Luca Fiori got to her. In every way.

CHAPTER FOUR

"I THOUGHT we were storing the furniture in the Green Conference room, and the rest in the storage area off the south corridor."

Mari looked up, knowing she looked harried because she was. Yesterday she'd received another letter. She'd hardly slept last night thinking about what it said. Hating how the past still had this hold over her.

Now, this was the second time Luca had interfered with clearing out the lounge. He stood beside her, not a bead of sweat or hair out of place or a wrinkle in his trousers or his chocolate-brown shirt, calmly issuing edicts.

"You said the *other* conference room. The Mount Baker." She knew it was hard for Luca to remember, but all the rooms were named after peaks in the Rockies and she was determined to use the proper names, not identify them by color.

"The Mount Baker is being used for meetings."

"When did that happen?"

"When I scheduled them."

She took deep breaths to hold on to her temper. Everything was in flux and it was starting to get to her. Now he was changing his mind and she was just supposed to go with it.

"You scheduled them? Why not use another room?"

"Because the company I hired to renovate our spa wanted a room where they could use a projector."

Her head spun. A spa? They'd have to discuss that one, but not now. Now she had a dozen employees moving furniture and putting it in the wrong place.

"Luca, do you think you could get out of my hair long enough to let me do my job?"

"Certainly. I have calls to make."

Cool as a cucumber. Mari scowled after him. Luca was infuriating. Nothing seemed to faze him, and she could hardly keep her balance.

She put her hands on her hips and took a moment to redirect the staff—again—that was emptying the Athabasca Lounge of furniture. Once they were back on track, she sighed and pushed her hair out of her face. Her twist had long since been in tatters and she'd resorted to anchoring it with an elastic, except pieces kept escaping and getting in her way.

The more she knew of Luca, the more she didn't quite know what to make of him. Her playboy image of him had been reshaped and a new version in its place. Oh, the charm was still very present, hard as she tried to ignore it. But she was coming to discover that he was used to getting his own way. Only a week after his arrival and already things were changing, shifting, strange workmen appeared from out of nowhere, and she was signing for deliveries. He'd definitely taken charge. She certainly couldn't say he was lackadaisical about the job. He seemed completely committed to the Cascade.

And he'd definitely taken to ordering *her* around. This morning was just another in a long line of commands he'd issued. She caught sight of him now, talking to a man in dark green trousers and a lighter green shirt. A laborer of some sort by his uniform. Luca's arms spread wide and his eyes danced as he spoke to the man.

She had to admit things were never dull anymore. Every day there was a new discovery to be made. Adjustments to be made. The lack of routine threw her off her stride. And when he went at something, he did it all the way. That included making her chafe at the bit at being ordered around when she was, in fact, the manager of the hotel.

Yet all it had taken was one bit of information to make her feel like a complete fraud. To make her return to being the scared little girl she'd been for so long.

A crash echoed through the room and she jumped, pressing a hand to her heart. Her head jerked toward the sound as a flash of a memory raced before her eyes. Glass after glass, shattered against the kitchen wall as she cowered in the corner. Her heart pounded against her ribs and she struggled to keep her composure. This was not *then,* and no one had thrown anything at her. A table holding glassware had been bumped, sending vases and pitchers teetering over the edge. That was all.

With a sigh, she grabbed a spare box and started picking up pieces. But when an employee passed by and said, "Sorry, Ms. Ross," she lost her grip on the thin edge of her control.

"Sorry? Why can't you watch where you're going?" She huffed out a disgusted sigh. "Look at this mess!" Her eyes stung suddenly, mortified. How often had those words rung in *her* ears? Her regret was instant.

The girl faltered, her lips twisting. "I'll help you clean it up."

"Is something wrong?"

Mari looked up from her crouched position. Luca stood over her, his usually smiling lips flat with disapproval.

"Besides careless employees breaking hundreds of dollars of crystal? Not at all."

The girl's eyes filled with tears at the dressing down and Luca's gaze fell on Mari, steady and disapproving. Guilt slipped through her; she knew she'd been out of line with her tone. She was manager of the Cascade. The staff had to know she was still in charge. But that didn't mean she had to be a bully. Her, of all people! Shame reddened her cheeks.

"Lisa, I'm so sorry." She looked up at the young woman, mollified and contrite. "I know it was an accident. Please… my tone with you was inexcusable."

"I *am* sorry, Miss Ross! Please let me do that. It was my fault."

"Go back to work, Lisa, and don't worry, we'll get this straightened out." Luca's voice was calmly reasonable, completely unemotional and she hated him for it. She tried to ignore his body just behind her and focused on putting broken pieces of glass in the box. And all the while a voice in the back of her head was chanting, *he's out, he's out, he's out.*

"Yelling at the staff isn't the way to get them to work better."

Oh, as if she didn't already know that. Apparently he didn't understand that the constant changes and adjustments needed meant that she was juggling twice her normal workload. He had no idea of the other stresses she was under, that kept her awake into the dark hours of the night. "I don't need *you* to tell *me* how to do *my* job."

"Leave the glass and come with me."

"God Luca, stop ordering me around!" She looked up again and let her eyes flash at him. Frustration bubbled up and out. "I'm tired of it. You've bossed me around all week."

His eyes darkened and she knew she'd pushed the anger button. Crossed the insubordinate line. Dread curled in her stomach. How many times had she let this happen? How many times had she let her temper get the better of her and then have to pay the price for it? All the lessons she'd learned flew out of her head when he glared at her.

"In my office, if you please." The words were gritted out.

"No." She nearly choked on the word, and backed up a few steps. But the thought of following him into his office to be called to the carpet for her actions was more than she could bear. She would cry. She would beg, like she had so many times before. And then she'd hate him for it.

"Ms. Ross, unless you want this to happen in front of your staff, you'll come with me now." His voice was dangerously low and smooth. Sweat pooled at the base of her spine as she rose and brushed her hands down her trousers.

She could handle this. She could. Luca was not Robert. He couldn't be Robert.

She followed him into his office and while he sat in one of the chairs, she stood by the door. A means of escape if she needed it. Logically she knew this was just an argument. It didn't mean…but it didn't stop the physical reaction. That fight-or-flight response. And she knew her choice was always flight.

"Mari, *what* is going on with you?"

"I don't know what you mean." She worked hard at not fidgeting with her hands.

"You've been out of sorts all week. Tense, irritated. Short with the staff. What happened today was an accident, and you blew it out of proportion. The same as you did when Christopher put the Maxwells in the wrong room. It was easily fixed."

"What happened today was staff being careless. And I know I snapped at her, and I apologized."

"And the Mari I met a week ago, the one so concerned for her people, wouldn't have handled it by shouting at them."

She looked away. He was right. She was so tired of him being right. But telling him the truth—that the man who had terrorized her was out on parole— that just wasn't an option.

"We need to be able to work together, Mari. We need to be on the same page."

She took a breath and exhaled, glad of the diversion from the real problem. "Maybe that's it, Luca. I don't feel that we're working together. You're giving orders and expecting them to be carried out. I haven't had one single input into what's happening here other than writing the memo to staff."

"You've been at every meeting Dean and I have held."

"Yes, but why bother? I never get to say anything or weigh in on discussions. The two of you go on your merry way and leave me out of it. All you do is issue orders about what you want done and when. Never mind increased workload or trying to make adjustments. What's it like, Luca, being at the top? You don't have to try to finesse the little changes to keep things running as smoothly as possible."

"I beg your pardon." His voice was stiff and formal. "I believe you said that was your job."

Oh, the man made her blood boil. Using that against her. "It is. But I'm still only one person and the volume of work has increased significantly. And you also said you wanted my input."

"Is there anything we've done you don't agree with?"

She paused. The truth was she *did* like all the ideas and changes so far.

"That's hardly the point. You've set me up as your traffic cop, directing people here and there. Seven impossible things to be done before breakfast is even served."

"If you can't handle the job…"

Panic threaded through her. This was what she hadn't wanted to happen and she'd been working day and night so it wouldn't. She needed this job. She wanted this job and the life she'd built back. She'd thought that she would simply have to work extra hard for this short period of time and all would be well. And it had only been a week and they were at each other's throats.

"I can handle the job. *My* job. But I'm only one person, Luca."

"So you're angry at me, and not with Lisa. You're

not the only one putting in long hours, Mari. I don't ask anything of my staff that I don't ask of myself."

"Then perhaps you expect too much."

"Yet here we are. And I'm not the one throwing a tantrum."

She let out a sound of frustration. "You are infuriating!"

A slow smile curled up his cheek. "So I've been told."

The cajoling did nothing to lighten her mood, only darkened it. Her tone was biting. "Probably by your legions of swooning women."

"Legions?" He smiled at that, too.

"Would you stop smiling? I read the magazines."

He laughed then, a rich lazy chuckle that did things to her insides. She immediately hated him for it. She was trying to stay angry! It was easier than actually *liking* him. Watching him work the past week, she'd come dangerously close to admiring his enthusiasm and dedication.

"Oh, Mari, are you jealous?"

"Hardly." She said with so much contempt she thought he must believe her. Her? Jealous of his women? Why on earth would she be? His eyes sparkled at her and she ground her teeth. It wasn't fair that his shirt today matched the exact rich brown of his eyes. *So what,* she thought. He had nice eyes, he was sex-on-a-stick gorgeous. But he drove her crazy. She wasn't in the market for a man, and even if she were, it wouldn't be a dictatorial womanizer like Luca. She curled her lip. "Trust me, Luca. I have no desire to be a notch on your bedpost."

Her heart trembled as the words echoed through the office. What did she think she was doing, challenging him!

His smile faded. "That's clear enough. And let me be clear, Mari. If you have an idea, a problem with anything happening here, you need to speak up. My education did not include mind reading."

But she wasn't used to speaking up. She was used to order and routine. She'd gotten where she was by being good at her job, not by running over the top of people to get there. She knew what happened when you rocked the boat.

Slowly, in the silence, she felt her anger dissipate. "I don't like arguing."

"I love it." He smiled suddenly, the corners of his eyes crinkling. She stared at him. He loved it? Her stomach tied in knots at the very thought of confrontation and she was completely stressed now that she seemed to be dealing with it nearly every day. And he claimed to enjoy it?

"How can you say that?"

"Don't you feel better?"

"I don't follow."

He stood up, but leaned back against his desk, stretching out his long legs and crossing them at the ankle as he braced his hands on the edge of the wood. "Having an honest, open argument is much better than holding frustrations and resentments inside. Clears the air. It doesn't fester. It's healthy."

"I'm sorry if I don't quite get the concept of healthy confrontation. To me there's nothing healthy about shouting at each other, hurling insults. In the end someone always ends up getting hurt because one person doesn't know when to stop." She said it all in one breath, but couldn't look at him while she did it. And she steeled herself, willing away the shaking that happened every time she thought about Robert. Knowing he was out there somewhere, and free.

Something clicked in Luca's head. A seed of an idea that was suddenly so clear he didn't know why he hadn't put two and two together before. Maybe because he'd been so focused on his job that he hadn't given it priority.

Mari had been hurt. Someone had hurt her and now she was afraid.

It made sense. He'd missed the signs but he could see them now. Her aversion to touching, to arguing. The way she'd looked at him in the attic, the way she stood now, by the door, like she was ready to flee. The way her eyes wouldn't meet his, keeping her distance. In his family, arguing was something done often and passionately, the same as loving. One didn't negate the other. He couldn't live life with his sister and father and not argue, it was part of who they were. But he'd been right about the loving, too. As much as he chafed at his father's control of Fiori, it didn't stop the love between them. It was the love that had made them safe. But he could see now that somehow, with Mari, someone had taught her differently. Someone had taught her that love hurt.

But he couldn't broach the topic. They hardly knew each other. He was her boss, and it would be crossing a personal line. But he couldn't help but wonder what—or who—had made her so afraid. The last thing he wanted was for her to be afraid of him. He was no threat.

"Mari, I'm sorry. I certainly didn't mean to upset you. We've both been under some stress." He decided a little insight into himself wouldn't hurt, to put her at ease. He smiled at her. "I'm Italian. In my family we argue as passionately as we love each other. We know that we'll be there for each other, no matter how much we disagree. I didn't think that perhaps not everyone is the same way."

She turned her eyes on him and he was caught for a brief moment. The same as that day in the attic, her eyes shone like gray dawn at him and he saw there was much more to Mari than he'd imagined. He could see the pain. The pain she thought she kept hidden inside behind the wall she'd built around herself. He'd seen that kind of ache before. In his father's eyes, and in his sister Gina's. It was, he realized, the look of the death of hope. As hard as he'd tried over the years, he'd never been able to make that look go away for them completely. "I'm sorry," he repeated.

Her voice was soft. "And I lost my temper before and owe you an apology."

"Accepted."

They couldn't go on being at each other's throats all the time. It wouldn't be good for the hotel, or the staff, or for either of them. And the first step was for him to offer her an olive branch. "It's a beautiful day outside and from what I hear, one of the last. Let me treat you to lunch. Now that we've cleared the air."

"I don't think that's a good idea."

He began to hold out his hand, but pulled it back. He normally would have taken her fingers in his, but he remembered her aversion to touching.

"I'm offering a truce, Mari. I would like us to be friends. I'd like for you to be comfortable enough with me that you can feel free to offer an opinion. You know this area. You know the staff far better than I. You are a great asset to the Cascade, Mari, and it won't be good for either of us if we cannot find a way to work together. We can't have more arguments like we did today. It's counterproductive."

"Luca, I appreciate the gesture, but I have a list of phone calls to make, not to mention the actual running of the hotel. We're shuffling so many things around I'm having to adjust everywhere…"

"You need to take a break and come back refreshed. A little relaxation now means higher productivity later. Besides, I'm hungry. You have to eat. I insist."

For someone who didn't like orders, she seemed to understand them well enough. He saw her capitulate as her shoulders slumped slightly.

"Oh, all right."

He smiled, his mind already working. She was still uptight— they both were. This wasn't finished. The best plan was to get away from the hotel altogether, somewhere they could meet on middle ground. He wanted her to look at him without the guard she put up all the time.

He wanted her to trust him.

"Meet me in the courtyard. And bring a sweater."

"The courtyard?"

He went to her, reaching around and opening the door. "Fifteen minutes, *si?*"

She stepped outside into the courtyard, her boots making dull sounds on the cobbled walk. He was standing by a bench to the right, by the remains of the rose garden. Now that most of her anger had dissipated, she felt that unfamiliar crawl again. No matter how hard she tried, he pushed her buttons. Either one extreme or the other. And she didn't know which was more difficult—fighting with him or fighting the attraction that seemed to be budding.

He'd been completely right this morning, and then had offered an apology. To her recollection, no man had ever apologized to her before. Damn it, she was starting to *like* him.

He was talking to another couple—Mari recognized them as the Townsends, the anniversary couple—and it took a lot of effort not to turn around and go back inside. The morning, combined with their argument and then apology had left her exhausted and off balance. She wasn't sure what to say.

He'd apologized for arguing with her. He wanted to establish a better working relationship. And she knew by Christmas he'd be gone back to Italy and everything would go back to normal. It was only for the short-term. It all should have made her feel much better. But it didn't.

She approached with a smile. "Good afternoon."

"Ah, Ms. Ross. You've met Mr. and Mrs. Townsend?"

She appreciated Luca using her surname. She held out her hand. "It's nice to see you again. Are you enjoying your stay with us?"

Mrs. Townsend beamed. "We are. It's just beautiful here. And that dinner the other night…what a lovely way to celebrate our anniversary. Thank you so much."

Mari smiled. "You are very welcome. Such a milestone deserves special treatment."

"Indeed it does," Luca remarked.

Mr. Townsend noticed the picnic basket. "We're keeping you."

Luca smiled back. "Not at all. We're just testing out a new program we may implement, and the day was too beautiful to waste."

Mr. Townsend lifted a hand in farewell. "Enjoy then. And thank you for a memorable week."

"Congratulations," Luca and Mari said together, then looked at each other and smiled. As the Townsends walked off, Mari lowered her gaze as she felt her cheeks bloom.

"Thank you for coming."

"When the boss gives an order…" She chanced a look up. Their brief encounter with the Townsends only served to remind her of how personable he was. He remembered details, and knew how to put people at ease. She admired that; it was a quality she'd never mastered. She tried hard to ignore the older couple's smiles as they'd seen Luca holding the picnic basket. A warmth spread through her at the thought of them paired together.

He laughed shortly. "I thought you said I wasn't to give orders anymore."

"I don't think you can help it…it's in your nature. Where are we going? I'm hungry." She wasn't, really, but knew her body needed nourishment. More than a muffin and several cups of coffee, which was all she'd eaten so far today. The sooner she got this over with, the sooner she could get back.

He stood to the side, revealing a wicker picnic basket. "I had the kitchens put together a meal for us. And if you'll follow me, I have the car waiting to take us to our destination."

"A picnic." Mari wasn't sure if she should be happy or aghast. What would the staff say if they went gallivanting away on a picnic for two?

"Colleagues and friends enjoying a late fall day. Nothing shocking about that."

"Can't we eat here?" She looked around. The gardens were filled with benches and grassy expanses. It would certainly be more seemly. She was still trying to grasp the fact that he'd referred to them as *friends*.

"Mari, we're changing more than cosmetics here. Remember what I said to you that night at dinner?" He turned slightly, lifting his arm to encompass the gardens. "Remember the Romance. Restoring the Cascade is more than furniture and fabrics. It's also services, special touches. Imagine being here in this town, with the man you love. Venturing out on a sunny day to a mountain meadow where you share lunch, a bottle of wine."

With the man you love. She *couldn't* actually imagine it. She couldn't imagine letting herself be in love, giving someone that much power. This…this magnetism to Luca was just that. Magnetism. She stared at his chest, which was a mistake as she couldn't help wondering what was beneath the sweater he'd put on against the brisk autumn chill. She had to deflect the intimate mood somehow.

"As long as you don't share lunch with the bears. Or elk. They can be mean this time of year, you know. The elk."

Luca's jaw tightened; he wasn't amused. "Fine, Mari. Don't go if you've not a mind to."

He picked up the basket.

She closed her eyes, frustrated. "Luca, wait. I'm sorry. I just find this…awkward. I'm not used to catered picnics with my boss." That wasn't all. The very idea of being alone, secluded…it made her feel closed in, defenseless.

"I thought we could both use an hour away from the hotel. A chance to see something else. I've hardly seen any of the townsite yet. I thought you would be a good tour guide."

Mari's level of discomfort grew. Here at the hotel they were surrounded by staff. It was her turf, as well as his. But this picnic, it was completely organized by him and she had no idea where they were going. She wasn't great at following someone else's plans.

"Maybe I could pick the place, then," she blurted out. At least then she would feel more comfortable. "As you said, I do know the area."

He carried the basket and she led the way out to the new luxury car he'd purchased for the hotel. The most senior of their shuttle bus drivers had

taken over chauffeur duties and he opened her door
with a smile, "Ms. Ross."

"Thank you, Charlie," she murmured, sliding in,
sinking into the soft leather seats.

Luca slid in beside her after placing the basket
in the trunk.

"Where to?"

"To my place, if you could." Mari leaned forward.
"You remember the way?"

"Sure do, Ms. Ross."

"Your place?"

She felt Luca's eyes on her and she nodded
without looking at him. Her place, her turf. A tiny
element of protection. "Yes. I'd like to change into
jeans and a sweater. And introduce you to someone."

CHAPTER FIVE

IT WAS only a matter of a few minutes until the car pulled up outside a stone cottage, perched on the side of a hill dotted with spruce trees and shrubs. Charlie opened her door and she got out. "Would it be too much to ask you to wait for us, Charlie?"

"You're the boss, Miss Ross."

She smiled at him then. She was glad Luca had chosen him as their driver. He'd been driving shuttle bus for several years, and she'd always enjoyed his anecdotes about his grandchildren. Charlie was one of the few men she felt very comfortable around.

"You may as well come down, too, Luca. We'll walk to the spot from here."

She walked down the stone path to her door while Luca retrieved the basket from the car. As soon as her feet hit the veranda the barking started and she smiled. As she opened the door, she called out, "It's just me!" and was greeted by happy licks and tail wags.

Tommy. Her companion, her protection, her one bright spot of unconditional love.

"You wanna go for a walk, boy?"

More butt wiggling as his tail beat a furious pace. Then he spied Luca at the top of the path and leaped out the door.

"Tommy!"

For once he ignored her command, reached the top of the path and with a loud bark, jumped up on Luca, planting firm paws on Luca's chest.

What next?

Luca rubbed Tommy's blond ears. "Aren't you handsome." He called down to Mari. "I didn't know you had a dog!"

At least he wasn't angry. Even if she was mortified that her dog had met him with more exuberance than he should have.

"Tommy. Come."

At her sharp command, the Labrador slunk back down the stone steps to where she stood on the veranda. "Lie down."

He dropped by her feet.

"If he's that well trained, I can only assume you whispered something in his ear as he went out the door." Luca's teasing voice came closer as he descended to the cottage.

"I'm sorry about your sweater."

"It's not even dirty. Besides, that's what laundry service is for."

"Tommy, stay." She left the dog on the porch floor and opened the screen door. "I'll just be a moment."

"So this is who you wanted me to meet?"

She paused. "Yeah. I figured if we're going to be lunching outside, it would be a good chance to let him out for a run. He's such a good boy, staying in all day and waiting for me." She knelt down and rubbed the top of his head. "It would be a big treat for him to get out in the middle of the day for a romp."

"You don't leave him out in your garden?"

Mari ceased patting and looked up. "I know it sounds cruel, leaving him shut up all day. And I probably could leave him out, but I don't trust the bears." She leaned her forehead against Tommy's warm neck. "I don't know what I'd do if anything happened to him."

He was also a level of protection for her. Nothing would hurt her while Tommy was close by. He wasn't vicious by any stretch, but he was big and he was loyal.

"We'll wait for you, then. Enjoy the outside and get acquainted." Luca put the basket down and sat on a deck chair, rubbing Tommy's silky ears in his fingers.

Mari went into the bedroom and pulled jeans and a soft sweater out of her closet. It felt strangely intimate, undressing and knowing Luca was only a few steps away. She slid the jeans over her panties, pulled the sweater over her head and re-did her ponytail.

All the while aware that he was out on her porch, with her dog and a picnic.

This could technically be classified as a date.

She sat heavily on the bed. No, it was a working lunch, that was all. A break from the craziness that had become the Cascade and testing out guest services. They could eat and still classify it as work. They could forge a truce of sorts. That was what Luca had said, right? That he wanted to be friends. She was torn. She wanted friends, she did. And yet the idea of getting close to people frightened her. She wished she were different. That she could leave the past where it belonged, behind her. That she could shed all the hurt and fear and live a normal life. Instead she tied herself into knots over the mere thought of being alone with her boss for a simple lunch.

Mari wasn't prepared for the tumbling feeling in her belly when he came into a room. She'd spent so long on her own, focused on getting her life together that it was a new and unsettling experience. Bringing him here today wasn't an accident. Knowing Tommy was with them—between them—would help. He was her reinforcement. Charlie would be waiting here, with the car. She would not be alone. And perhaps with this one lunch Mari and Luca could finally set a consistent tone. Perhaps they could come to some agreement on how to deal with each other during the coming weeks. He was right about that. They had to find a way to work together.

"Mari? Are you all right?"

She startled at the sound of his voice. She'd been

daydreaming for several minutes, leaving him to his own devices on her veranda.

"Coming," she called out, standing and smoothing her clothing. He hadn't made this into anything other than lunch. It was Mari who was off balance. She either sniped at him or stared at him stupidly. It was her imagination running wild because he caused her temperature to rise a little bit each time he was around.

And because she hadn't felt like this in such a long time the novelty was jarring.

She met them back on the porch. "Let's go. Tommy, come."

The dog fell in step at her heels, while Luca carried the basket, and the black Cadillac rested down the hill from them.

She led him across the lane and up a small, single track path. Little traffic ventured along here, but she could always see her little cottage just below. The grass was drying, golden in the noontime light. When she reached the crest of the hill, she stopped, picked up a stick and threw it a short distance for Tommy, who bounded off and then brought it back, tail wagging.

From the crest of the hill they could see down the valley. Her cottage and their car lay below them; the hollow was cradled by spruces and pines and the ever-present poplars and birches that were rapidly losing their plumage. The nearly round leaves scattered everywhere, forming a golden carpet, while the air held the sharp tang of evergreen. "Is this okay?"

Luca put down the basket and reached inside for a blanket. "It's perfect."

She sat down on the blanket, throwing the stick for the dog again. "We won't have many more days like this," she murmured, feeling the sun warm her face. "I'm surprised it's held on this long."

"Then we must make the most of it." He began unpacking the basket. "Tomato bocconcini and peppers, marinated lamb and minted potato salad, and I'm not telling you what's for dessert because good girls eat their vegetables first." He laid out real china and silverware along with their parcels and said, "If you'll serve, Mari, I'll pour the wine."

For a few minutes they busied themselves with laying out the picnic. Mari sat with her legs crossed, arranging the meal on the plates. Already she could feel the stress of work ebbing away and filled with a newer, sweeter problem—the fact that she was, indeed, enjoying his company. She tilted her chin up to the sun, letting its warmth absorb into her sweater. She was glad to be here with him, sharing something as simple as a picnic on a fall day. But that was as far as it could go. She had to remember why she had come. To establish some sort of truce. Some sort of equilibrium between them. She wasn't capable of anything more.

"Fresh air and good food does wonders for

stress." Luca's voice came from beside her and she turned to look at him, squinting against the sun.

"This is one of those times I'm going to have to admit you're right again." She handed him his plate, smiling. "I didn't realize how tense I was. I've been so focused on trying to get everything accomplished with the same number of hours in the day."

Tommy had played himself out bounding through the grass, and collapsed in a contented heap a few feet away. "I haven't been doing this with him enough lately. I need to or he's going to get fat and lazy."

"Everyone needs downtime like this. Outside, peace and quiet, something simple and restorative. It's what I hope people find at the Cascade. A break from the…what's the term… the rat race. Time to smell the roses. For some, this is a way of life."

"For someone like you, you mean?"

He smiled and took a bite of bocconcini. "Someone like me?"

She gave him a significant look and he grinned. "Oh, you mean the idle rich."

She took a drink of the mellow chardonnay, enjoying the light teasing between them. "I will concede that you are definitely not idle. You've proved that this last week."

"You thought I was?"

She looked down over the valley. "Oh come on, the golden son of Fiori Resorts? I've read the magazines, you know. Life handed to you on a silver platter? Fancy cars and fast women… or is that fast cars and fancy women?" She couldn't stop the teasing quiver of her mouth.

"Either way," he admitted dryly.

"You're incorrigible," she giggled, leaning a little sideways and jostling his shoulder.

And sighed into her wine.

"Have I been pushing too hard, then?"

She eyed him carefully. Had he? He never looked tense or flustered or tired, but she knew for a fact that he was up and working by the time she arrived in the morning, and just last night when she had gone home late, he was still on his computer in his office.

"I don't think you've been pushing anyone harder than yourself. But maybe the Cascade staff isn't used to that pace."

"Staff like you?"

She put off answering by nibbling on her potato salad. But his gaze remained on her face and she swallowed.

"I didn't get where I am without putting in the hours," she replied. She was tired. It was no secret. But part of the fatigue was due to the fact that things were changing and she was unsettled. She was under stresses he knew nothing about, nor would he. She was waking more in the night than she usually did. The nightmares had returned. She was looking over her shoulder. It meant she started most days already at an energy deficit.

"I wouldn't have asked so much of you if I weren't sure you could handle it, Mari."

And she couldn't help the warmth that spread through her at his words of confidence.

"And I thank you for that. As well as thanking you for realizing I needed a breather."

When Mari pushed away her plate, Luca reached into the basket one more time.

"I know I probably shouldn't have, but I got them to sneak in dessert." He removed a ceramic pot and a spoon, held them up.

"You thought of everything."

"Not everything. They only sent one spoon."

She stared at the single utensil. What sort of game was he playing? She thought he'd simply hand her the dish and that would be it. But instead he dipped the spoon in and out, a smile playing on his lips.

"I told you that there was simple beauty to be found. That the Cascade meant an *experience,* more than providing a service. What if we weren't running the hotel? What if we were guests? We wouldn't be thinking of whether or not this was profitable, we'd be thinking of how wonderful the afternoon has been. We'd be opening our senses, our minds. We'd be thinking of ourselves and enjoyment and not worrying about a thing."

Her heart tripped over itself as he held up the spoon, rounded with crème brûlée.

"Close your eyes, Mari."

Oh God. This wasn't putting up boundaries at all, or establishing a status quo. It was blowing it all to smithereens and she wasn't sure she could do it.

He held the spoon, waiting. She was caught by his warm gaze, as lazy and seductive as the creamy concoction on the spoon.

And she closed her eyes.

The cold spoon touched her lips and she instinctively opened them. Felt the cool richness of the dessert enfold her tongue. Smooth, soft, sweet.

As the spoon left her lips, she opened her eyes.

Luca dipped the spoon again, but this time tasted it himself, his gaze never leaving hers.

"It's good," he murmured, presenting her with the spoon once more.

The spoon that had just been in his mouth. It was silly that the thought would have such an effect on her, but it felt like seduction. She opened her mouth and let him feed her, feeling more and more like she was completely out of her mind and her element. She didn't know what to do with romance. And this was clearly romance.

"It really is exquisite." Not only the dessert, but being here with him, and she had to find a way to divert the mood. It was sheer craziness that she'd let herself fall under his spell, but she knew what came next. Before she knew it they'd be kissing. The very idea made her tremble, from want and fear. She was

not equipped for an affair, and she was smart enough
to know an affair was all there would be with Luca.
He was a limited time fantasy, and she couldn't
afford to buy into it.

She had to bring it back to the business of the
hotel somehow. Mari started fussing with plates and
silverware to avoid being fed any more of the
decadent dessert. "I think we could develop a selection of picnic items."

Luca helped himself to one more spoonful and
Mari forced herself to look away from how his lips
encircled the spoon.

He put the dish down and picked up his wine. "Interesting idea. Maybe offer a selection to choose
from. Don't want the bocconcini? Have a shrimp
and rice salad, perhaps. Herbed chicken instead of
lamb. Gunther's chocolate terrine instead of crème
brûlée. What do you think?"

What Mari thought was that test driving a sports
car wasn't the same as owning one, and doing a
dry run for a romantic picnic wasn't like being on
one. But…the potential was still there and she
could use her imagination. Especially after the last
few moments.

If she were in love with Luca, and he with her, and
they were in this setting, eating decadently, growing
lazy on fine wine…

A couple in love would be romanced. And they'd
end the afternoon in a very different way than she

would with Luca. And that would be part of the Cascade experience.

And how would such a couple end the day? Mari's hand paused over the dishes. Perhaps they'd return to the hotel and order in room service. Or they'd dress in fine clothing and have dinner at the best tables, dancing on the gleaming parquet floor with the scent of fresh flowers falling around them. He'd smile and hold out his hand, his brown eyes shining down at her because she was so lovely…

"Mari?"

"I think that sounds wonderful," she answered, fussing with the blanket beside her feet, knowing that such a scenario was not possible, even as longing suffused her. A chill blew in with the breeze and she shivered. She had to stop thinking of him this way. Everything would go sideways and there'd be no graceful way out. If she couldn't even stand his hand on her arm, how could she possibly relax enough for there to be more? She was simply tired and her defenses were down. She was muddled from the wine. It had to be about the Cascade, not about them.

But she'd have to go back to the hotel with Luca and the thought of walking back through the lobby with him and a picnic basket sent quivers through her stomach. They didn't need rumors circulating amongst the staff. Even over something as innocent as a picnic. She desperately needed to put the tone back to business.

"We could do a variation on a winter picnic. Soup in a thermal container, bread and cheese, hot cocoa and a dessert."

Luca grabbed the basket and began repacking the dishes she'd gathered into the basket. "That's brilliant. We can adjust it and make it seasonal. The Rocky Mountains in winter. See, I knew you'd catch on."

Maybe to the concept, but definitely not the execution. Falling in love and being romanced was fine for some people, but not for her. Not anymore. She looked over at Luca's profile as he wrapped the now-empty wineglasses in linens to keep them safe. Never would she let someone take over her life so much that it wasn't hers anymore. She wouldn't give anyone that much control ever again.

It was just as well Luca was only here for a few weeks, certainly he'd be gone by the new year. In a way that made him safe, too. Any attraction she felt wouldn't matter. She wouldn't have to worry about feelings deepening and things being awkward. She just had to hold out until he was gone and she could get the life she'd built back. Her safe life. A life where no one had the power to hurt her again.

"Why don't you take the rest of the afternoon off?"

Luca stood, holding the basket. Mari hopped up, grabbing the blanket and folding it into an imprecise square. It was tempting. But her car was still at the hotel and she'd dallied enough today. There was still work to be done and she didn't want to take advantage. It was important for her to end the day with their work relationship at the fore, not the lazy intimacy of the picnic.

"Thanks for the offer, but my car's still there anyway."

They walked back down the hill, Tommy trotting happily ahead. The stress headache that had been lurking behind her eyes was completely gone. Perhaps Luca was right. She did need to relax more. She certainly had relaxed with him. Perhaps too much.

"I'll be back in a few moments," she murmured as they reached the cottage. She put Tommy in the house and checked his water bowl before locking the door and leaving again.

Charlie drove up and opened the door for her. Luca got in again, and her eyes were drawn to how the fabric of his trousers hugged his thigh. As the car pulled away and back down the mountain, she leaned back and studied him without being obvious. He wore his clothes like he belonged in them. He was at ease, comfortable with himself, and it came across as confidence. She blinked slowly, wishing she had that sort of self-assurance. She agonized over every piece of her wardrobe, yet he seemed so at home in whatever he wore, whether it was jeans and a T-shirt, or dress trousers with his trendy shirts. She imagined he'd be equally handsome in evening wear. Looking like she'd imagined earlier. A picnic like today, then an elegant dinner, only it wasn't guests she envisioned but the two of them. Stepping out on their dance floor, with her on his arm…

"We're here."

Mari heard the words but the fabric against her cheek was soft and warm. She snuggled into it further.

"Mari, I hate to wake you but we can't sit in the car forever."

The voice intruded again and she realized it was Luca. Then she realized she was leaned against the breadth of his arm. It was wider and stronger than she'd anticipated. And his scent came through with each slow breath.

She sat up abruptly, putting distance between them. Her last thought had been of him dressed in a tuxedo. Now she was intimately couched in the back seat of a luxury car with him. She edged over further. "I fell asleep."

His smile was lazy, indulgent. "You did. Almost as soon as the car began to move."

"I'm so sorry."

"Don't be. It's perfectly all right."

Embarrassment flamed in her face. "But it's an eight-minute drive from my place."

"Obviously you were tired. And relaxed. Shall we?"

Charlie had opened the door with a bland look on his face.

She got out into the refreshing mountain air, its bite going a long way to clearing her head. Luca said something to Charlie and then he touched her elbow and they walked toward the lobby doors together. Just before they reached the entrance, Luca quipped, "Don't let it get around that my company put you to sleep. I have a reputation to uphold."

As she let out an unexpected splutter of laughter, he opened the door and held it as she passed through. He followed her in, both of them chuckling.

"Luca."

Both their steps halted as they turned together toward the voice. Mari stared at the most beautiful woman she'd ever seen. She was the picture of class, elegance, style. She was dressed in a trouser suit of dove-gray silk with matching heels, her nearly black hair flawlessly styled around a heart-shaped face, dominated by brown eyes and the thickest set of natural lashes Mari had ever seen.

"Gina."

Mari could only gape as Luca dropped the picnic basket and crossed the floor with long strides, gathered the woman up in his arms, and swung her around.

When he put her down, she laughed out loud. "I missed you." She cupped his face and kissed one side, then the other.

"And I you. What are you doing here?"

"I came to see you. Aren't I allowed?" The smile on her face was filled with teasing.

The Italian accent was clear. Mari didn't understand the spurt of jealousy she felt nor did she like standing in the middle of the lobby looking daft. She

bent to pick up the abandoned basket. The picnic had
been two co-workers, not lovers, so there was no
reason for her to be jealous now. She had work to
do. She'd return this to the kitchen and go back to
her office.

As she bent down, the woman spied her. "Luca,
introduce me to your friend."

Mari straightened slowly.

"Of course." Tugging the woman's hand, he led
her to where Mari was standing. She felt more
stupid by the second, embarrassed. Here she was,
the manager of the hotel, in jeans, a sweater, with
her hair in a windblown tangle, talking to a woman
who looked as though she wouldn't be caught dead
in such a state. Not only that, but the scenario was
so predictable it even made *her* wince. Of course
Luca would have a girlfriend. She should have
foreseen. Instead she was caught looking provincial
and awkward. A caricature.

"Gina, this is Mariella Ross, the manager of the
hotel."

Gina held out a hand. Mari shook it and then
looked down. She'd expected soft, perfectly mani-
cured hands with sculpted talons for nails. Instead
the hands were gentle but plain, with neatly trimmed
nails painted only with clear polish.

"Mari, this is my sister, Gina."

Mari's flush deepened. Oh, would she ever stop
feeling stupid?

Gina's light laugh echoed. "Luca, I'm offended. You didn't tell her you had a sister?

Mari looked up but to her relief Gina's eyes held nothing but humor. She should have seen the resemblance straight off. The same color eyes, the same shaped lips. "He hasn't said a word about his family."

Gina swatted Luca's arm with her matching clutch purse. "Of course he didn't. Men. All about work."

"What are you doing here, Gina?"

Luca stood by Mari as he asked the question again. This time Mari noticed the brunette's eyes dim as she said something in rapid-fire Italian and Luca answered back, his cheeks suddenly drawn. Mari wrinkled her nose. Happy, carefree Luca? He looked positively thunderous.

"Is something wrong?"

Luca spared her a glance. "A family issue."

"I'm sorry. I'll leave you two alone." Mari picked up the basket again, prepared to leave.

"Mariella?"

Mari didn't have the heart to correct Gina. It didn't matter right now. There was clearly something going on between Luca and Gina that any explanations of her name could wait.

When she paused, Gina continued. "I do hope you'll join Luca and me for dinner tonight. I'd love to hear about your plans for the hotel. Luca thinks he has the only eye for decoration, but he underestimates his sister."

"Perhaps you need time to catch up. You needn't feel obligated."

"It's no obligation at all. Tell her, Luca." Gina smiled up at her brother, who was scowling back at her.

Luca turned his head and stared down into her eyes, his expression softening. Despite her fears and misgivings, she wanted to hear him say the words. It made no sense. What they'd shared, first in the attic, and now on the picnic, scared her. She would be foolish to want more. She should refuse and go the other way. Instead she wanted him to ask her. Wanted to hear him say he wanted to spend time with her. How on earth had this happened?

"We would both like it," he said, and her gaze dropped to his lips for a brief second. "I would like it. Please, come."

"I will."

"Wonderful." Gina smiled. "It will give me a chance to wear the new dress I bought in Milan."

Mari felt her insides blanch. She couldn't go like this. This wasn't her business supper of a week ago where a skirt and blazer were the order of the day. There was suddenly a standard to uphold and she wasn't sure she was up to it.

"If I'm joining you, then I must excuse myself. I have so much to do…if you'll excuse me."

She didn't dare look up into Luca's face. If she did she'd be caught. Instead she hurried away, mentally assessing her wardrobe and wondering what on earth would be suitable.

Luca watched her go. She hadn't said as much, but from her blush she'd thought Gina was his lover. A wrinkle formed between his brows. Interesting. Perhaps Mari wasn't as immune as she pretended to be.

"She's lovely, Luca. I can't imagine why you haven't mentioned her."

Gina's voice diverted him and he spun back around. "There's nothing to mention. Unlike yourself. Let's go to my suite so you can tell me why you're here, Gina."

Once in the rooms, Luca went to a cabinet and opened the door. "Wine or brandy?"

Gina smiled. "Neither. Oh, it's good to see you. You travel too much and I never see you anymore."

He led her to the sofa, then sat on the arm of a nearby chair. "Father sent you?"

"Father sent the sculpture you asked for. I chaperoned it."

Luca held his annoyance. He hadn't seen Gina in weeks and he didn't want to argue.

"And you, I suppose, had to get your finger in the pot."

She grinned cheekily. "Darling, it's what I do best. I'd be a horrible sister if I didn't help at least a little with our newest acquisition."

"I thought you were busy with *your* newest acquisition." He slid off the arm and down into the cushions, crossing his ankle over his knee. "How is my new niece?"

"Growing. And her brother is turning my hair gray."

"Good. You deserve it."

She snorted out a laugh. "I have missed you, Luca."

"And I you. But you have Angelo and the children now. You didn't need to come."

"I still have an interest in Fiori, Luca. Father sent me with the sculpture and to see if you needed a fresh set of eyes. And resources."

"You need to be with your family."

"I left the children with Carmela, the nanny, at Father's. Traveling with two small children…" Gina shook her head. "It will be a grand holiday for them, with Carmela to keep them in line and Papa to spoil them. It makes me feel needed. Something of my own."

"And where is Angelo?"

"He is in Zurich, seeing to a new project. He will be back in a few days, and then Carmela and the children will go back to our villa. You worry too much, Luca."

Luca smiled, though his heart wasn't in it. Gina tried hard to be the exception. She insisted she and Angelo had found each other and now they had two beautiful children. Yet he'd always had the feeling that Angelo wasn't good enough for her. He had a difficult time believing it was enough to last. He couldn't help but wonder if down the road his sister was in for heartbreak. The same way their father had been.

Perhaps he was just being overprotective. He always had been where Gina was concerned.

Gina yawned, covering her mouth with a hand. "I'm sorry. It was a long flight."

"You are exhausted, Gina. Why don't you nap now." He stood and urged her down onto the plush cushions. "You don't want circles beneath your eyes tonight, or to be yawning through dinner. You can rest here, since I have work to finish downstairs. When I get back, I'll wake you and we can get ready, hmm?"

"And discuss the Cascade, don't forget." She winked at him. "*Grazie,* Luca."

"*Prego.* Rest now." He took the blanket—the same one he'd wrapped over Mari's arms—and laid it gently over her as her lids drooped.

His fingers grazed the soft blanket and he remembered Mari's eyes, closed, as he'd fed her crème brûlée. Remembered the feel of her, warm and soft against him in the limo today as she'd slept. He'd wanted to slide his arm around her and pull her on to his lap, feel her curled around him.

She had no idea what drove him. No idea why he worked so hard to prove himself. But Gina's comment about wanting something of her own made sense to him. He wanted to prove himself, to step forward and take a larger role at Fiori. His father had shouldered all the burden of the company, and family, as he and Gina had grown up. Luca had worked hard to take some of that burden, and now he just wanted what was his due.

In the beginning he'd thought it would be fun to make Mari see life was more than a balance sheet. It had seemed like a game. And admittedly he was good at games. But it had backfired. He hadn't counted on feeling attracted to her himself.

CHAPTER SIX

WHEN she walked into the room it was like someone punched him in the solar plexus, strangling all the air from his lungs.

Mari wasn't Mari tonight. She deserved the fullness of her name. She was Mariella. Every inch of her, from her hair to her toes, was elegance and shy sexuality. He hadn't known she could look like that. He had imagined what would happen if she let her hair down and left her tidy suits in her closet. But even that image had fallen woefully short.

"She is beautiful, Luca. An ingénue."

Gina's voice interrupted beside him as they watched Mari speak a moment to the hostess, a smile lighting her face.

"She keeps me on my toes."

"There *is* something between you then." She put her hand on his arm.

He shook his head. "No, Gina. She's the manager here and she's good at what she does. We work together. That's it."

Mari turned from the hostess and made her way to them. Luca tried to ignore the thrumming of his pulse at the gentle sway of her hips. Mari had legs. Yards of them, it seemed. Navy silk draped and clung in all the right places in the wrap-style dress, revealing shapely calves that curved elegantly into matching strappy heels. The neckline rose up from a V to cover her shoulders with barely an inch of strap.

"I see how you look at her, Luca. Trust me, you'll be happy that I'm here to free up some of your time."

Luca tore his eyes from Mari's image and glared at Gina. "If you think you're going to hang around here and be a thorn in my side…"

Gina smiled sweetly. "Dear brother, I consider it a family duty. She looks at you the same way."

Mari stopped in front of them and smiled, and for a moment his heart stopped.

"I hope I haven't kept you waiting."

It was Gina who replied when Luca remained silent. "Not at all. We just arrived ourselves. I had a refreshing nap and now I'm ready to sample your chef's delights."

Luca moved to pull out Mari's chair first.

"Thank you," she murmured, and he caught the first scent of her perfume.

"That dress is stunning. You have fabulous taste, Mari." Gina smiled disarmingly. "I hope Luca's not bullying you into making all *his* changes."

Mari smiled. "Thank you. And he tries, believe me."

Luca sat down. "I'm very fortunate to be sitting with the two most beautiful ladies in the room."

Gina laughed lightly. "Only the room? Mariella, I think we should be insulted."

But Luca's eyes had locked with Mari's. She'd left her hair down and his fingers itched to touch it, to be buried in the mahogany richness of it. It curved around her face and shoulders, and as she brushed a little of it back, he caught sight of her necklace, a silly little creation of silver and sapphire leaves.

He wanted to lift her tiny hand and press a kiss to it, but he knew she'd frown on it. "I can see I won't stand a chance with the two of you."

Mari smiled and her eyes twinkled at him. "Somehow I think you can hold your own."

Luca ordered champagne and sat back, listening to Mari and Gina speak as if they'd known each other forever. But Gina had always had that way about her. Open and interesting. She had the grace and ease about her that brought Mari out of her shell like he hadn't been able to. And seeing Mari relaxed made her shine. She was open in a way she'd never been with him.

They were partway through the second course when one of the waitstaff approached Mari with a problem.

"I'll get it, you enjoy yourself," Luca said, beginning to push back his chair.

"No, I will." She smiled easily. "It is my job, after all. I won't be a minute."

He stood while she rose from her chair and sat again, watching her as she followed the staff member toward the kitchen.

He looked over at his sister, who kept insisting she was happy in her marriage. Was Luca the only one who could see what she was doing? She kept saying Angelo was her happy ending and he wouldn't be the one to shatter the illusion. He wanted it for her, after all they'd been through as children when their mother had abandoned them. He remembered holding her when she was little, when she cried for their mother in the night and didn't want Papa to hear. Remembered the summer he'd suspected there was something between her and Dante. But then Dante had gone to Paris with him and when they'd returned, she'd been engaged to Angelo. And he'd known she was trying to make up for the life they hadn't had and he'd been powerless to stop it.

He'd been by her side during the darkest time in her life. He'd been the older one. He'd understood more. He sincerely hoped Gina wasn't in for the same heartbreak again. *He* certainly wasn't in the market for a fairy tale happy ending. Neither were the women he usually dated, and that suited him just fine.

When Mari returned, he let his gaze fall on her as she and Gina spoke of the internal workings of the hotel business.

Mari was different. He couldn't explain it, but

somehow all the jaded thoughts from the past faded away when she was near. There could never be anything permanent between them, but the brittle sense of skepticism he usually carried dissolved when she was around. He'd seen her eyes light up as she spoke to Gina, laughing easily in a way he hadn't seen before.

It was mesmerizing. This was Mari, unguarded. He'd wondered if she could ever be this way. Now he wondered if she could ever be this way *with him*.

"Luca, you must dance with me."

Gina issued the command and Luca sighed. "Gina."

"You know you want to. Besides, who else am I going to dance with? I don't see you for months on end. And this really is a quick trip."

Mari looked at Luca and a reluctant smile crawled up her cheek at his mulish expression.

She'd smiled more today than she could recall smiling in a long time. Seeing Luca being bossed around by his little sister was enjoyable. She'd gotten so used to him giving orders that she was delighted he knew how to indulge his sister.

"Ah, the family guilt," Mari teased him. "The same no matter what nationality you are."

"Oh, we Italians are particularly well-versed in it," Gina replied jauntily. "Let's go, Luca."

Mari watched, wishing she had the natural ease and grace that the Fioris seemed to possess. She'd

insisted that Luca dance with Gina, and it was fun
watching them. He took a wide step and spun his
sister around, and the sound of her tinkling laughter
reached Mari's ears. This was a man she could warm
to. Like she had during their picnic, dinner with
Gina seemed to have released the tension he'd been
holding in. It made him even more attractive. She
wet her lips. Not in a million years, would she have
expected to be feeling a physical attraction to a man.
Especially not now, when she knew Robert was out
there, and free.

She knew her mother must know that he was out
on parole, and for the first time, she wondered what
Anne was doing, where she was. After the trial
Mariella had walked away, not looking back. She
couldn't. But through the years and silence between
them, there was no denying that her mum had had
to deal with the same thing. Perhaps even more
than Mariella, she must be feeling like it wasn't
ever truly over. For the first time in a long time, she
felt sorry for her mother.

Breathless, Gina and Luca returned to the table.
Gina sat but Luca looked down at Mari. She forced
a smile, but she knew it was too late. He'd seen her
melancholy. His eyes softened with concern and he
held out his hand. "Mari? Dance?"

Mari stared at his extended palm. Could she? The
scene was eerily close to her musings just before
she'd dozed off in the limo. But now, faced with the

reality, her stomach twisted in knots at the thought of being held so closely in his arms. She wanted to dance, she discovered. But she didn't trust herself to handle it. Not when the mere thought of Robert caused the trembling to start. The last thing she wanted to do was have the proximity of his body trigger her panic. For once, she was unsure of her own reaction and she hesitated.

"Go on, Mari, dance. Luca's actually a very good dancer." Gina narrowed her eyes at her brother. "But if you repeat that, I'll deny it."

Mari let out a breath and carefully put her hand in Luca's as she rose from her chair. Immediately she felt the warmth of his hand radiate up her arm. "I suppose I could dance, once."

He led her to the dim floor. Her heels echoed on the parquet and he turned, pulling her gently into his arms. She felt like she was in a dream. Gone was the Luca of before, the man of casual flair, of style and flirtation. In his place was a gentleman. He seemed to know how she felt about touching and kept a polite distance between them. Knowing he did it out of respect for her drew her to him in ways that his innate charm never could. Even so, one hand was warm at her waist, and he cupped her right hand within his, a perfect fit.

He was dashing tonight, dressed in a dark suit, his tie precisely knotted, his hair slicked back, reminiscent of the golden age days he so wanted the hotel to represent. The song was slow and jazzy, the singer's voice smooth and rich like melted caramel. Luca's arm cradled her waist as he lifted their joined hands close to his shoulder. "Relax," he whispered, and their feet started to move to the music.

Unlike when he danced with Gina, now Luca didn't say a word. Mari swallowed, closing her eyes and letting the music in, guiding her feet around the intimate floor. Their steps grew lazy and Mari drew his scent in, that expensive, man-scent that she knew she'd always recognize as his. Their bodies were closer now than before, and the trembling in her body wasn't fear. Perhaps it was, she thought, but not fear of her safety.

Fear of Luca and the way he made her feel. Because he was making her feel things she'd never wanted to feel at all. Vulnerable. Wanting, dear lord. Wanting to give a part of herself to him, rather than closet it away.

His hips swayed against hers and she longed to rest her cheek against the fabric of his dinner jacket. His hand slid up her back, leaving a warm trail in its wake. This then, was what it felt like to feel cherished.

Breath caught in her throat. She'd felt safe once before only to have it go very wrong. As much as her heart told her she was safe with Luca, she couldn't be sure. Couldn't take that risk. She couldn't survive it again.

It was very good he was a short-term complication.

The music ended and Luca pulled away. "Let's walk."

"But Gina…"

"Gina has gone to bed."

His voice was warm in her ear and goose bumps erupted on her skin. She jerked her head to look back at their table, but he was right. It was empty, save for the remnants of their dessert.

He took her hand and led her to the balcony doors. As they stepped outside, the cool autumn air assaulted them and Mari welcomed it. It would clear her head. This was crazy.

The music was muted as Luca shut the doors behind them. Mari walked to the railing, resting against the sandstone and looking down over the valley. The moonshine glittered over the winding river.

"Why did Gina leave? I thought she was enjoying herself."

Luca's voice came, deep and smooth, from behind her. "I believe she thought we could use some time alone."

Everything in her dropped to her feet.

"Luca, I don't think this is a good idea." The words came out strangled, shaky.

"I know it's not."

She turned her head at his response. Having him admit it was wrong somehow made it all the more tempting. He was standing a few feet behind her, so tall and strong with the façade of the hotel behind him.

"Then what are we doing?"

"I brought you out here because…" He paused.

"Because…" Her voice was a whisper.

He turned away, abruptly. "I'm sorry, Mari. It was a mistake."

Disappointment cooled her warm skin, and she wrapped her arms around herself. Evenings on the terrace were very romantic, except for when it was only a few degrees Celsius above freezing and one was wearing a sleeveless dress. And when the man in question turned away. It amazed her to realize she didn't want him to.

She shivered and he looked back at her. "You're cold." Without hesitation, Luca removed his jacket and came forward, draping it around her shoulders. For a moment she wondered if he'd pull her into his arms as his hands gripped the lapels. But he released them and stood back.

His shirt stood out, crisp and white in the moonlight and Mari thought again how perfect he looked. And how looks could be deceiving.

"I thought you said Gina had children and couldn't come."

"She does. They are at our father's, with their nanny."

"I see."

"Do you?"

She tilted her head to look up at him. "Not really." She smiled. "What is clear is that you love her. And she loves you. I—" She broke off, wondering how much was safe to tell him. "I envy you. I never had a brother or sister, or much of a family at all."

"Where's your family now? What about your mother and father?"

He came to stand beside her at the balustrade and they looked out over the hulking shadows of the mountains together. "I never knew my father, and I haven't spoken to my mother in several years."

"Does it have something to do with why you're so afraid of me?"

She bit on her lip. She couldn't look at him, not now. He wouldn't understand about Robert, and her mother, and it would only make things awkward between them. Her feelings might be changing, but Luca definitely wouldn't be interested in someone with so much baggage. He had a father and sister, and his whole business was based on family. They were from two very different worlds.

"It doesn't matter, Luca."

He linked his fingers with hers, and her heart soared. In ten minutes he'd treated her to more tender, caring touches than she remembered getting in her lifetime.

It would be too easy to fall for him.

"What about you? You must have a girlfriend…or girlfriends…lurking about somewhere."

She thought he'd take his hand away from hers, but he didn't. "Not really."

"Oh, that's right. You like playing the singles game. Do you really think you can do that forever?"

He did pull away then, and his jaw tightened. She wanted him close to her so badly she knew she had to push him away. "I don't particularly believe in love, Mari."

She smiled, but it was barely a curving of her lips. "That makes two of us."

His eyes, deep and dark, rested on her. The scent of his cologne wafted from his jacket so that she felt like he was touching her even when his hands were in his pockets. "What did it for you?"

He would walk away, but perhaps that was best anyway. He didn't need to know the story; he wouldn't be here long enough for it to matter. "When the one person who should love you doesn't, it tends to shape you whether you want it to or not. So I came here, and built my own life. It's all I have, Luca."

He nodded slowly. "And you think I will take it away from you."

She confirmed it by simply remaining where she was, her gaze steady on his.

"I won't."

"I won't let you."

That tripped a ghost of a smile.

"What about you, Luca? Why don't you believe in love?"

"My mother abandoned us…all of us…when we were children. I heard Gina crying herself to sleep every night. I saw my father's anguish…and yet he still loved her. She divorced him and he gave her a settlement, but not once in all these years has she come to see Gina, or me. Or father. She walked off to a whole other life."

"You haven't seen her since?"

"Not once. Not even when Gina was married, or when her children were born."

"I'm sorry, Luca." Mari's heart ached for him. She knew what it was to feel insignificant in the eyes of a parent. "But your father…"

"He did a wonderful job raising us, and running Fiori. But in the absence of her, Fiori became his bride. He's fierce about keeping it under his control."

Mari reached out and touched his sleeve. "He doesn't trust you."

"He thinks he does."

Luca wanted more. He wanted something for himself. Perhaps they had more in common than she originally thought.

"So you came here to prove something."

He nodded, again slowly. She was mesmerized by the motion. The whole evening felt somehow like she was waking from a nightmare, complete with a sense of the surreal. He had touched her, and she hadn't flinched or been afraid. He was only here for a short time, and somehow being with him helped. She'd be a fool to question that, wouldn't she?

"I never, never want to be in the position that

father was. I don't need any great psychoanalysis. I don't trust love, not the long-lasting kind."

"So you satisfy yourself with temporary flings."

"I tried something more once. It only ended up hurting both of us. It's better this way."

"What happened?"

Luca hesitated and she sensed his hurt. Perhaps she shouldn't pry. But an *open* Luca…it wasn't likely to happen again. She wanted to know. It was so unlike her, but she wanted to know about him, the little details that had shaped him into the man he was. Here in the starlight it was like she couldn't get enough.

Luca met her eyes. "I had an affair with a woman I worked with. It didn't end well."

"Who did the ending?"

His lips tipped up slightly, but there was little warmth in the pseudosmile. "She did. Unofficially, and for someone else."

The quirk of his eyebrow told her as much as any words could. Her lips dropped open. "You mean you caught her with another man?"

"Indeed."

"I see."

"It is just better for everyone to keep things upfront and honest. No unrealistic expectations. Don't you agree?"

At least they were on the same page. It should have been a comforting thought, but it wasn't. Not in the least. Her brows puckered. She didn't want a relationship, nor a fling. And yet there was something within her that wanted to explore this thing that was growing between them.

"What are you thinking, Mariella Ross, standing there in the moonlight?"

She swallowed. Held his gaze not because she wanted to but because she could not look away. "What are *you* thinking?"

His voice was rich silk. "I think I'm about to make a big mistake." He took a step closer.

Mari saw immediately where this was heading and alarm bells started pealing madly. "Luca, I don't think…".

"Relax, Mari. I'm not interested in falling in love. Love only results in people being hurt."

She should be feeling relief. Those were her thoughts exactly. She didn't understand why she was slightly deflated at his statement. "We can agree on that, then."

She backed up against the stone railing, closing her eyes.

"Mari."

When she opened her eyes he was directly in front of her, his warm gaze steady on hers.

"I know you've been hurt badly." Her eyes widened but he continued in that same, soft, hypnotic tone. "I can see it in you. I realized it after that day in the attic. I won't hurt you, Mari. We'll keep our eyes open. I promise."

He lifted his hand and his fingers disappeared beneath her hair. Her breath caught as she fought against the urge to lean into the pressure of his hand. Luca kept his promises. Eyes open.

"Beautiful Mari. I cannot deny there is something between us. I feel it. You feel it, too. We both felt it today, in the meadow. I could see it in your eyes. But the difference is we set the limits. We set the boundaries."

"I can't sleep with you, Luca." It came out on a rush of breath.

A smile teased his mouth. "Perhaps a kiss."

He was close enough now that she had to tip her chin up to meet his eyes. It was a struggle to keep them open as his fingertips moved through her hair. "Kiss."

"Surely you've kissed before?"

Mari's insides trembled. She had, but not for a very long time. Not without utter fear.

"A time or two."

His face was so close his breath warmed her cheeks. Her fingers tightened around the edges of his jacket. Surely, if she could make it through a first kiss, it would all be fine. "Kiss me, Mariella."

Their gazes held for a second. He was waiting for her, she realized. He understood she'd been hurt and he was letting her make the first move. It was unexpected. She was used to him bossing her around. Now he was giving her the power and it made him even more difficult to resist.

She leaned into his hand, tilted her face up, and with her heart in her throat, touched her lips to his.

For a split second she let them rest there, testing. Their eyes were open, and the connection between them was so strong it rocked her core. His lips were warm, soft, waiting. She let go of the jacket and rested a hand against his heart and she felt the thunder beneath her palm.

The simple movement changed everything. Her breath came out in a rush as Luca's hand commanded her head, tilting it gently to the side and he opened his lips. Her lashes fluttered shut. The kiss was deliberate but soft, easing into the passion slowly, building the fire with teasing nips.

For the first time since leaving her old life behind, she threw caution to the wind, wrapping her arms around his torso and pulling him closer.

The moment she did it, everything changed. His hand swept from beneath her hair and dragged her close. His tongue swept into her mouth and she wilted against him. The jacket fell from her shoulders to the floor of the terrace and his hands warmed her skin as they roamed over the bare flesh of her arms.

Glory.

He broke off the kiss, resting his forehead against hers.

Mariella pulled out of his arms, immediately feeling the cool air and the bite of cold reality. "Thank you."

His eyes glittered at her knowingly. "Thank you?"

She had to take a step backward. She'd been swept away in the magic of the moment and had forgotten. She was supposed to be afraid. She was supposed to keep personal distance. She was not supposed to let herself be vulnerable. She could not… a sob built in her chest. She could not allow herself to *feel*.

She wanted to deny it, but he'd know she was running away from it, and him. And to acknowledge it had affected her deeply was to take things where she didn't want them to go.

"As you said, there's a certain amount of chemistry." She lifted her chin, daring him to contradict her.

Instead he laughed, reaching out and grazing her cheek with a knuckle.

"You are a strong woman, Mari. You do my grandmother's name justice. She was a strong woman, too."

Mari swallowed. Coming on the heels of the kiss, she was seeing a whole new side to Luca. Whether he recognized it or not, he carried around his own scars, ones indelibly scraped on his heart.

She turned away, leaving him staring at her back as she rested her elbows on the balustrade.

"You remind me of her." He paused for a moment. "Why did you not correct Gina when she called you by your full name?"

Mari shrugged. "It would have been rude of me. We'd just met."

"But you didn't mind being rude to me."

She heard the dull sound of his shoes on the stone floor as he came closer. "You can take it."

"I appreciate you being kind to my sister. Annoyance that she is."

Mari held her breath as his hands appeared on either side of her and he leaned closer, not quite an embrace, but with his chest leaning warm and secure against her back.

"Mariella."

Mari's eyelids drifted shut. The soft way he said it was sweet seduction. But it was no better as his image appeared behind her eyes. The way he looked tonight, the way the expensive cut of his suit emphasized his physique, making him look like a movie star from bygone days. Too much like the man from her dreams. She had to resist him. Had to. This was madness. She was supposed to be afraid. Repulsed. She wasn't supposed to be feeling like this.

His lips touched the back of her neck and she quivered. Tilted her head without thinking, allowing him access to the gentle curve.

His arms tightened around her and his wide hands rested just below her waist, their warmth seeping through to her skin.

"You didn't correct me just now."

"No, I didn't." The words came out on a breathy whisper.

How could she possibly explain that the way he

said it sounded different? How could she do that without making this more than either of them wanted?

"You would honor me if you let me use your given name, Mariella. It was the name of a woman I loved very much and I've missed the sound of it on my lips."

Her lips parted but no sound came out. How could she refuse him now? They'd moved this far out of the realm of strictly business and she wasn't at all sure how it had happened. She only knew they had a connection. Knew that somehow tonight they had shared more than simple family history. Somehow, in between the main course and this moment, she'd started to trust Luca. She'd let him in, whether he realized it or not.

She swallowed, opened her eyes and turned so that she was still in his arms, but facing him.

"You really mean that. That's not a line, is it."

He shook his head. "My *nonna* was very special to me. And she would have liked you, Mariella. She'd have liked you very much."

Mari would have answered, but Luca bent his head and kissed her again, sending all her words scattering into the starlight.

CHAPTER SEVEN

"You wanted to see me, Mari?"

Mari looked up as Luca stopped at the door to her office. The smooth sound of his voice sent flutters over her skin and she shook them away. The intimate whispers of last night weren't real. Today was what was real. She had to set the tone.

Last night had been a fantasy, dressed up in finery, gazing at stars from balconies. But today they had to get back to business. Gone was the dashing movie-star gorgeous hero, and in his place was the real Luca. The one in regular trousers and trendy shirts that showed off the lean physique of his upper body. She couldn't stop the visceral reaction to his appearance any more than she could stop the instant knowledge that kissing him had been a terrible mistake.

No matter how wonderful.

"Luca, come in."

He ambled into the office. She'd been here early, had made sure of it. Yesterday had been a one-off.

Gallivanting on picnics and romantic dinners. Being held in his arms and kissing beneath the stars. That wasn't reality. Reality was the Cascade and the job at hand. How easily she'd forgotten. How completely he'd managed to distract her.

He took a seat across from her desk, crossing an ankle over his knee. "I'm sorry I wasn't here earlier. I had breakfast with Gina. And she doesn't rise early. If I had known you wanted to see me…"

"You'd have what?" She folded her hands on top of the papers neatly arranged in front of her.

"I'd have made myself available."

The dizzying thought of Luca making himself *available* to her spun through her veins, the anticipation of possibility seducing her away from her goal. No one had ever made her a priority. No one had put something off for her before. But for all she knew that could just be pretty words.

"You're here now. And since we were out yesterday afternoon, there's a lot to catch up on."

She began explaining about contractors and unions while he was looking at her. She stuttered over a word, realizing he was gazing at her face, her neck, the buttons on her jacket. He wasn't paying attention. Scratch that. He was paying too much attention!

"Luca, are you listening?"

He straightened his shoulders and leaned forward a little. "Intently."

Oh, indeed he was. She blinked, forced herself to

keep to the topic at hand. "I needed to see you about these invoices." She held out a sheaf of papers. "Luca, those numbers can't possibly be correct." He'd mentioned upgrading the spa facilities, but the numbers coming in didn't make any sense to her.

He glanced down at the sheets. "Yes, that's right." He tossed off the matter. "What's on your schedule for this afternoon?"

Her face blanched as she ignored his last question and focused on the fact that he'd said the invoices were accurate. "Look again. That decimal point can't be right."

He handed them back to her. "It's all in order, Mari."

She tapped her pen against the blotter, unsure of how to proceed. Surely he could see the folly in laying out so much money in addition to all the other things he was adding. She had seen the bill for the new draperies for the Athabasca Room and had nearly fainted. It had gone way beyond what they'd agreed when they'd laid out the budget. Now this…

"This is not what we budgeted. And you went over our budget for the drapes by nearly thirty percent!"

"It was a great price for a much higher quality fabric. Gina found it and…"

"Gina?" Mari stopped fidgeting and put down her pen. Fighting Luca was difficult enough. But now she had two Fioris to keep up with. Gina had delivered a sculpture, but she also did much of the interior design detail for Fiori Resorts. Trying to keep Gina from spending them into the ground was yet another tick on her to-do list. She couldn't take them both on. She took a deep breath.

"I told you she was persistent."

Then she caught a hint of a smile at the corners of his mouth.

And she remembered that mouth on hers.

And his hands on her skin.

And how everything else had vacated her mind during those moments.

He tried to charm her and then ignored the plans they'd already set out for the Cascade. He'd done it more than once already. This was one time when his charm wasn't going to work.

They had set out a plan. A plan to enhance the hotel while looking after her staff. It was up to her to keep it, especially if he kept looking at her in *that* way.

She ran a hand over her hair, though not a strand had dared to escape her precisely arranged knot. "Luca, we can't possibly afford the draperies, let alone the spa. The plans already mean incorporating other space into this expanded spa vision. Need I remind you how expensive that restructure is going to be? But this…this is beyond exorbitant. It's *criminal*."

"I assure you it's not." He continued on, unfazed. As cool as could be. "This isn't a third-class hotel, Mariella. It's a *world-class* hotel. That means going with the best." He lowered his chin and pinned her with his gaze. "Fiori always chooses the best."

She heaved a sigh, ignoring what she knew he intended to be a disarming compliment. "There must be a way to trim these costs. You promised no shutdowns or layoffs. With something of this magnitude…you won't be able to avoid it. The money has to come from somewhere."

"I won't?" He grinned suddenly. "Oh, Mari, that sounds like a challenge. And I do like a challenge."

Her heart slammed against her ribs, but she narrowed her eyes. He hadn't had to say the words to know that he considered *her* a challenge. And she didn't like that, not one bit. She'd been a challenge to Robert, she understood that now. She'd been independent and free and she knew the challenge had been for her stepfather to break her. And he'd done a fabulous job of that, for a long time.

But last night she'd proved that his power over her wasn't absolute. She'd enjoyed Luca's touch. She'd come alive beneath his hands and had welcomed his kiss. And somehow that made her feel just a little bit powerful. She wouldn't be under anyone's thumb ever again. But she refused to be a challenge for Luca.

The trouble was, she *wanted* to trust him. So far he'd kept to his word about the changes to the hotel, despite his exorbitant taste. And the staff was, for the most part, happy. Luca had a way about him. Even when he'd explained to some staff that in order to stay, they'd have to do different tasks than was the norm, they'd greeted the news enthusiastically.

No one had been dismissed or made redundant. In fact, the whole place was running remarkably smoothly, considering.

And the fact that his sudden smile had her entire body warming didn't help, either. It drew her eyes to his mouth again. And that made her remember last night and how magical his mouth had felt on hers.

For once, in those moments in Luca's arms, she'd forgotten Robert Langston even existed. And he'd been a constant for the last twenty years, present or not. For once she'd felt sheltered and protected and not defined by what had happened to her before. The world had opened up for her in the moment she'd twined her arms around Luca's ribs. And it had been exhilarating and terrifying.

Now in the cool light of day, it seemed impossible. For nothing had really changed. Robert was still out there, and nothing could change the things he'd done to her, or her mother. Luca would still be leaving in a matter of weeks and her goal had to be the big picture. Wasn't that what Luca had said? And the big picture was holding on to this job that she'd worked so hard for.

"It's not a challenge, it's fact." She bolstered her argument with numbers. If they could just keep this about the hotel, and not about them, then she might stand a hope of keeping things clear and professional. "This invoice alone is for over a hundred thousand dollars."

"And every guest who comes out of our spa will feel like a million."

"I doubt it."

Mari watched as Luca ran a finger beneath his bottom lip and she remembered how their bodies had been close. How she'd shamelessly wrapped her arms around his ribs and pulled him in so that the warmth of his body pulsed through her. That couldn't happen again. A relationship was out of the question. Boundaries. He'd said they could set the boundaries. She wished he'd let her.

"Have you ever had a spa day, Mariella?"

"I've had facials and pedicures, sure." Once, when she'd first moved here and had treated herself. When she'd been reinventing herself.

"No, not that kind. The kind where you spend a whole day. You are massaged and buffed and polished from head to toe, so that when you're done you feel like you own an entirely new body."

She shook her head.

"You must. I'll talk to Gina."

Gina again.

She was losing ground quickly. Somehow this conversation had gotten away from the topic of expenditures and she had to bring it back.

"I do not have time for a spa day, Gina or not."

His smile was crafty. "But if you're with Gina, she's out of my hair."

"And conveniently, so am I." She raised her brows

so he knew she was on to him. "You made these changes without even consulting me."

"I *am* the owner."

Mari unclenched her fingers, relieved they were back to the safe topic of talking about the hotel again. "As I'm well aware." She smiled coolly. "I have to run these figures again, if they are, as you say, correct. Find a way to trim costs somewhere else." She didn't add that she blamed him for the extra work; there was no need. He never seemed to listen to her cautions about money. He simply forged ahead with whatever scheme he had in mind. And he was a great one for schemes.

"Mariella, you are going to worry yourself into the ground. Take the day. Enjoy it." He reached over and put his hand over hers. "You're no good to me or the employees here if you're out on stress leave because you've pushed yourself too hard."

Words seemed to strangle when she tried to talk and she paused. He wasn't goading her or criticizing. His eyes were sincere. He actually sounded like he cared.

He was so hard to resist when he was this way. It had been easier for her to deal with the work this morning than think about the what-if's with Luca. But he was here now and work didn't solve a thing. If anything it only served to increase her awareness of him. To highlight how often during the day they were together. To remind her of how much she'd lost herself in his arms last night. To remind her of how much she longed to trust someone, to have them fill that empty space she'd become so adept at ignoring.

Luca saw her face change, saw that little hint of vulnerability she tried to keep hidden. He recognized that look. Gina had had it, less now that she had her own family, but he'd seen it enough growing up. In his days here, he hadn't seen Mariella with any friends. She never talked about her family. She was, to his recollection, the most *alone* person he'd ever met. And something told him she had it that way on purpose.

It would be good for her to have a day with Gina. Moreover, it would get them both out of his hair for a blessed few hours so he could work in peace.

"I want to do this for you, Mariella. I want you to take the rest of the morning and treat yourself to a massage or a wrap or whatever you like." And he lifted her hand and kissed the back.

It was a mistake. The scent of her skin as he touched it with his lips made him remember the feel of her last night, soft and pliant in his arms. It had affected him more than he'd expected, but he'd been unable to resist going to her on the balcony. There was nothing brash about her, she had no agenda, and that set her apart from most of the women he escorted to various functions. But that wasn't all.

It would be very easy to care for Mari, to care too much. She seemed to need it, but he wasn't the one to give it. He would be leaving. She was different. He knew she wasn't the kind of woman to string along. And he didn't have it in him to give her anything more.

He dropped her hand and sauntered to the door. As he reached the threshold, he turned his head back. "Oh, if you could, be back at two-thirty. I've made us an appointment to see some artwork at a local gallery."

He shut the door behind him. Mari could never know that the attraction was becoming very real for him. It would complicate everything, and right now he needed to keep things simple.

At two-thirty Mari met Luca in the lobby.

"What, no Gina?" She'd left Luca's sister after their hot stone massages, refusing an invitation to lunch and instead working in her office, desperate to keep up with the workload.

"Gina sends her apologies, but Charlie has taken her back to Calgary to catch a flight home."

She caught the small furrow between his eyebrows. "Has something happened? Is it your father?"

"Why would you ask about my father?" The wrinkle deepened.

She looked up at him and put her hand on his arm. "You said her children were staying with him."

He sighed, and put his hand over hers. "No, it's not Papa. I rather think it's Gina and Angelo, but she wouldn't tell me."

"I'm sorry."

He put on a smile, though she saw through it to the worry. How long had he been shouldering the weight of his family? The thought came to her and she realized it fit. Luca felt responsible. He hid it behind a playboy-type façade, but after the way he'd spoken about his father and now his sister, she was sure of it.

"Let's not worry about that now. You look lovely. The spa clearly agreed with you."

Mari began to lift her hand to smooth her hair again but stopped. It had been wonderful, being fussed over and pampered. The stress had melted away with the heat of the rocks. She straightened her shoulders. "Thank you."

Yet she knew days at the spa and art shopping trips were things she couldn't get used to. She was Mari Ross of small town Ontario. Luca was Fiori of Fiori Resorts, used to glamour and a lifestyle very different from hers. It was understandable why she'd find that seductive. But it was also a reminder of why it was temporary.

Things like this simply didn't last.

When they reached the car, he leaned over and kissed her temple before she got in. "You look radiant," he murmured in her ear.

The spot on her scalp where he'd pressed his lips burned. He was acting as though they did this every day, for Pete's sake! All the feelings from last night's fairy tale came rushing back, and she tried to push them away. "It's the facial," she replied curtly, sliding over and buckling her seat belt.

They started with a small gallery tucked in behind Banff Avenue. Mari examined piece by piece, from soapstone sculptures to paintings to spectacular photographic work. As the visit continued, Mari felt like she was swept along with a whirlwind…only everywhere she turned, there was Luca, a few steps behind her. Always aware of him, the sound of his voice as he spoke to the proprietor. And using softer, more intimate tones for her.

It was hard to ignore him. Even if she really wanted to.

The saleslady was off to wrap a few of their smaller purchases to take with them, when Luca's hands draped over her shoulders, his fingers gripping the ends of her scarf. She jumped at the contact.

"Nervous?"

If only he knew. She wasn't sure she'd ever get used to sudden moves like that, even if it were Luca doing it. She breathed away the adrenaline rush. "I didn't see you behind me."

"This is lovely. The shade brings out the gray in your eyes."

"My eyes are ordinary blue."

She turned around to face him, expecting to see him smiling at her. Instead he was gazing at her, a serious expression clouding his eyes.

"Your eyes, Mariella, are anything but ordinary," he murmured, and before she could catch her breath, he dipped his head and touched her lips with his.

Her fingers gripped his arm as the gentle contact seared through her. His lips were soft as they explored her mouth, undemanding yet beguiling. He pulled away slightly, their breath mingling, waiting. Mari dimly remembered they were standing in the middle of a shop, but the noise faded away to a distant hum as she leaned in the inch and a half to kiss him again. Her eyelids drifted closed and Luca's free hand cupped her cheek.

The tenderness of it made her want to weep.

She hadn't realized, hadn't thought that the absence of affection had left such a huge hole. She hadn't wanted contact, or tenderness, or even kindness. Hadn't wanted to make herself vulnerable. She still didn't. But when Luca touched her this way, kissed her this way, like she was precious, she craved more of it. Like gentle, steady rain after a long drought.

He broke the kiss when a car horn honked outside on the street.

"Luca," she whispered. She'd come here to keep an eye on his purchases. To make sure he didn't outspend them again. To make sure she still had a say in the decisions being made.

Only it had backfired. She'd allowed him in and…dear God. She had *feelings* for him. Alarm thudded through her. She didn't do feelings! She had to keep things level. Luca wasn't really interested in *her,* she wasn't his type of woman. She knew that. Thank goodness one of them was thinking rationally.

Yet the thought that Luca wasn't interested in her at all left her crushed with disappointment. How could that be, when it was what she wanted? She didn't want to be closer to him, did she?

She lifted her confused eyes to his.

And was shocked to see her feelings mirrored back at her. He didn't say anything. But she knew. She knew she hadn't been alone in being affected by the kiss.

"There you go." The saleslady held out two bags, smiling like finding them in an embrace was a sweet secret. "The rest of your purchases will be shipped to the hotel."

Mari felt Luca's body behind her as she turned, the solid wall of him against her back as he put his arm around her, cradling her against him as he rested his chin atop her head. Mari wanted to beg him, *please don't be so kind.* And somehow she heard his unspoken answer: *Let me in.*

They left the shop and ventured on foot to the next, cradled between two restaurants on the busy main street. As he held the door for her, he murmured, "That's probably not a good idea, letting that happen again."

She stepped inside the door, the scent of vanilla and lavender teasing her nose. "No?"

"You're the manager, and I'm the owner. It wouldn't be good for appearances."

Mari nearly laughed. Luca, concerned about appearances? He was the one who wandered through the hotel in jeans instead of business suits. He was the one who asked for picnics and dinners and shunned anything traditional. He was the one who had his picture in magazines with a new woman on his arm every month, it seemed. "If I remember correctly, *you* kissed *me*."

"I believe you kissed me back."

Something in the last few days had caused something to break free in Mari. Instead of backing off she lifted her chin. "That's hardly the point now, is it."

"Fiori does have an image to uphold, Mariella."

Mari goggled.

"Who are you and what have you done with Luca?"

He only offered a tight smile in response. Mari stepped inside the gallery, immediately surrounded by pieces by local artists. She was secretly pleased he wanted to showcase local art. It was part of what the Cascade should be about. She was beginning to see that. This place was like no other place on earth. It deserved to be showcased as such.

She found some particularly interesting carvings

and when she looked up, Luca had moved on. She spied him in a side room, his hands in his pockets as he looked at paintings. She sighed. He was so…something. He was just so Luca. He made no apologies for it. The self-assurance was sexy, she realized. He'd been molded and shaped long ago, when his mother had left all of them. Now he knew who he was. She envied that.

When she reached him, he didn't look at her but simply said, "There are some wonderful pieces here."

For a moment she wondered about the cost of adding original art to the hotel. But put it aside for once. How could she worry about dollars and cents for her livelihood, when she'd splurged for perfectly selfish reasons today?

"I haven't been in here before."

"Don't you like art?"

He stopped his perusal and turned his head. The kiss they'd shared was suddenly in the front of her mind.

"I haven't given it much thought."

He turned back to the painting before him.

She found a bench and put down her bags. It was true. She hadn't had time for things like art appreciation. In the last store she'd merely followed his lead. She'd had more immediate needs, more pressing concerns. Like getting her life back. Taking charge. Moving forward instead of being paralyzed by fear.

And she'd done quite well, until that phone call. The one telling her Robert had served his time. Had

fulfilled his debt to society. It was no solace at all—
what about his debt to her? To her mother? Where
was he now? She could swear up and down she'd
rebuilt her life, but all she'd done was run. Run and
pretend. Now she didn't even know where her
mother was. If she'd run, as well. If she was even
okay. She'd gone years telling herself it didn't
matter, but now with Robert out of prison, her
thoughts kept turning back to the one parent she had.

Luca didn't get any of that. Nor would he. She
couldn't bring herself to explain it to him. Despite
their newfound closeness, she certainly didn't
know him, or trust him enough to fill him in on the
sordid details.

"Are you feeling well?"

"Excuse me?"

Luca was close to her shoulder. "Mariella, you are
pale as a ghost. Are you all right?"

"I'm fine. Show me the paintings you like." She
had to stop giving her stepfather any power. She'd
left that life behind.

He took her hand and showed her his favorites.
She dutifully nodded and commented. She ignored
the way he looked at her with his brows meeting in
the middle.

She bluffed her way through it, going through the
motions as best she could. The paintings he liked
were lovely, she could see that. They were mostly
landscapes, and with the Rocky Mountains being

their backyard, sweeping mountain scenes were prevalent. He favored those over the wildlifes or stills, she noticed numbly.

"Whichever ones you want will be fine."

He stopped in his tracks. "You have no opinion? You're not going to pull out your calculator and quote budgets to me?"

Mari swallowed. "You're going to do what you wish anyway, Luca. Why argue?"

"Because it's what we do best," he replied.

"I don't want to argue. The paintings are fine with me. They are very nice."

He stepped closer, his face puzzled. "But how do they make you feel, Mari?"

Feel? "Luca, it's paint on canvas." She didn't want to talk about how she felt. Today she'd felt like she was the girl she'd always wanted to be but hadn't been allowed. She could do what she wanted, buy what she wanted, feel what she wanted, and no one would punish her for it. She could take a morning off and no one would berate her. She could splurge on vanity and it was fine. The self-indulgence had been heady. Then reality had crashed in and she felt alone again, too weary to fight. Luca could make her forget, and it was wonderful while it lasted. But coming back to earth was a big thud and it hurt a little more each time.

"Yes, and the Cascade is a hunk of rock on a hillside. Even you know better than that."

"I'm afraid I'm not an art aficionado."

"You don't have to be to have feelings, Mari."

"Of course I have feelings!" she snapped.

She turned away, ashamed. Even-tempered, reliable Mari was suddenly all over the place. One moment she was sighing into his eyes and the next she was so overwhelmed she was biting his head off. She didn't know who she was anymore. He kept pushing at her, demanding things of her and her well-ordered life wasn't so black and white. She certainly didn't feel up to dealing with everything she was feeling.

He led her around a corner. "Look at these. Tell me what you feel. Let them speak to you. You'll know it when you see it."

She sighed, put upon. When he got like this, there was no deterring him. She had learned that already. She may as well humor him.

These were no landscapes. The paintings here were different, angled shapes and colors and impressions. Mari walked past, feeling no connections. Longing simply to return to the hotel. She was tired. She was drained. The whole day had been something special, but she doubted he'd understand how much it had meant to her. She'd felt a part of something.

Something based on a lie.

And then she turned a corner and saw it. Sweeps of blue with a brilliant core of red, exploding out from the middle in splashes.

It made no sense. But something about it spoke to her and she stepped ahead, lifting her fingers, coming close but not actually touching the canvas.

"Mari?"

Mari ignored his voice, but knew he'd been right all along. As hard as she'd fought, he'd been sure of himself. There was something inside her that Luca had set free, and it was right here in oil and canvas, looking back at her. She couldn't explain why, but she knew she had to have it.

CHAPTER EIGHT

"You like it."

She nodded, her eyes roving over the blend of paint and canvas. "I don't know why…it isn't even of anything at all."

"But…" he prompted.

She looked over her shoulder. "But it speaks to me somehow. I can't tell you what this is a painting of. I can only tell you that I feel connected to it somehow."

She turned back to the painting, her eyes drawn to the scarlet centre.

"So my Mari feels first and thinks later. I'm surprised." His words, his breath caressed the skin behind her ear, sending a delicious shiver down her spine. A warmth flooded her at being called *his*. It made her feel protected, like she belonged somewhere. And that with belonging, a sort of freedom she hadn't expected. She remembered how he'd described the view from his suite that very first day. Freedom. Little had she imagined then. Had she ever felt this way before, in her entire life? Like around every corner was an open door?

Had Luca changed her *that* much? How had he snuck past all her defenses so easily?

She half turned. "Surprised? Didn't you think I had feelings, Luca?" She did have feelings, so many of them that she refused to show the world. Letting people see inside her gave them *power.* It was much better to think, and wait. She'd been thinking a lot about Luca lately, and letting him in bit by bit, despite reservations. She couldn't seem to help herself, and couldn't pinpoint it any more than she could say exactly what it was about the painting that was so striking.

"Of course I did." He tucked an errant hair behind her ear. "I merely wondered what would finally make them break free."

She paused slightly, but she was growing bolder; dealing with him on a daily basis and having to stick up for herself had achieved that. She'd learned to trust him a little, and trust was uncharacteristic of her. And yes, he drove her crazy when he bossed her around. But he also touched her heart when he was gentle with her, as if he already knew her secrets.

After years of planning every moment, every aspect of her life, the ability to break out of the box was exciting. She wished he'd kiss her again, like he had on the balcony after dinner the other night.

Like he had just minutes ago. She looked up and met his eyes boldly. "What if I told you it was you?"

His golden eyes met hers. Clung. Without anything happening between them she felt the power of their earlier kiss. Swayed closer to him.

"Tell me why this painting." He broke the connection and faced the work of art.

She looked back at it, her heart thudding. The opportunity was gone but she hadn't imagined the link between them.

She wasn't sure why this particular painting spoke so strongly to her. It wasn't a painting of anything concrete at all, just a swirl of color. It wasn't of people that reminded her of someone, or mountains or lakes or places. It was a vertical rectangle with the color of twilight forming the background, the tones and shades swirling together in an ocean of blues. And bisecting it, a splash of deep, throbbing red.

"It's peace," she murmured, taking a step closer to it. Without thinking she reached down and took his hand in hers. "It's tranquillity and contentment and a thudding heart." When she looked at it, it made her ache. Made her hope, and that was something she'd given up on long ago. Hope was about the future, and she lived day to day. Luca would think that silly, she was sure, so she kept the last to herself.

Luca smiled, though he was unusually unsettled. He'd called her "his" Mari without thinking, and it shocked him to realize he thought of her that way. He'd meant to share the art with her, but it had become more very quickly and he felt the need to back away. The way she'd looked up at him, the way she'd credited him with her response, sent warning bells crashing through him.

It was all his fault. He'd ignored the signs and had told himself that he wasn't getting in too deep. Because he'd sworn not to.

He was about casual liaisons, but nothing about his feelings for Mari were simple or casual. It was a miscalculation he hadn't counted on. He'd be a liar if he didn't admit he had looked for an excuse to see her today. The kiss last night had affected him more than he'd expected. And he'd enjoyed knowing it had affected her, too, seeing her back in form when he'd arrived this morning. He'd taken pleasure knowing he'd gotten to her, seeing her trussed up in her suit and with her hair pulled back. Wearing her battle armor. Keeping him at arm's length. She had been right about one thing. He did enjoy a challenge.

But something had changed. It was more than enjoying her company, of matching wits. There was a connection with Mari that he hadn't anticipated. He felt it when she'd reacted to the painting. And when their eyes had met moments ago. And when he'd kissed her earlier this afternoon.

He took a step back, his brows pulling together as he stared at her back. "That's the meaning of art,

Mari. It doesn't have to make sense. It just needs to mean something."

She stepped up to the canvas and looked at the price. "That's insane."

He looked at the number. It wasn't exorbitant, but he remembered again that he was used to Fiori money and that such a sum was nothing to him. For someone in Mari's situation, he imagined it was quite different.

"Think of how it elicited such a reaction from you, and then try to quantify it. Can you put a price on that?"

"I can and have." She smiled, even as she gazed wistfully at the canvas.

He laughed, he couldn't help it. Mari was so charmingly practical. It reminded him how far apart they were and he took a little comfort in it. She was not for him. He was not for her. She was the kind of woman who looked for long-term stability, and he traveled around the world with his job, settling nowhere. This was just a blip on the radar.

"I could afford it, if I didn't eat for the next year. This is why art is in museums rather than living rooms."

She started to walk away. "I don't know why I was so struck by it anyway."

"You don't need to know why. Sometimes understanding takes all the magic away."

Once he'd said the words he considered them.

Mari moved down the wall, looking at the next pieces and he watched her. Maybe he was making this too complicated. An attraction did not a fairy tale make. And he was the last person on earth to believe in fairy tales. Gina believed enough for the two of them and he was happy for her. But it wasn't something he was willing to risk himself.

Gina had been young and full of her own grief at their mother's abandonment. Luca had been a little older. He had seen the toll it had taken on his father. He'd realized his father had truly loved his mother. Time and again he'd seen his father try to win her love only to fail, and in the end losing her had broken Papa's heart. Luca had never wanted to put himself through that anguish.

Maybe it was doing this job for too long that had him dissatisfied. Tired of the endless travel and rootlessness, of living out of a suitcase and only going home for holidays. Maybe that was what intrigued him about Mari. She knew her place and was happy in it.

He was smart enough to know it wasn't him she was enamored with. She was taken with the changes; with experiencing new things and it was breathtaking to watch her blossom. But he wasn't fool enough to believe it was him, as she said.

He wouldn't take it further than it had already gone, and in the end they'd part as friends. He'd return to Italy.

The idea didn't seem as charming as it had a few weeks ago. What was waiting for him at home seemed flat and lackluster now. More than ever he longed to break free and take his own place within the company. To step out of the shadows. To be Luca, not just the son and brother.

Mari returned to his side. "Have you finished?" She placed her hand on his sleeve. "I thought I'd do a little shopping of my own before the stores close. But if you're not...I can stay."

He wanted her to stay with him, he realized. And he didn't like knowing it. Didn't like knowing he'd somehow lost control of the situation he himself had orchestrated. He had to keep it to their original agreement. So that no one got hurt in the end. Maybe he wasn't looking for love, but he sure wasn't looking to hurt anyone, either.

"No, you go. I'll see you tomorrow."

"You're sure?"

He leaned over and on impulse dropped a light kiss on Mari's lips, wondering why in the world they tasted like strawberries. "I'm positive." He aimed a winning smile at her.

"All right then. Don't forget, we have a meeting in the morning with the landscape designer for our spring plans."

"I'll be there."

She squeezed his hand and grabbed her shopping bags. He turned around and looked at the painting again, but for the life of him he didn't see a beating heart.

Mari took a moment to roll her shoulders back and forth, easing out the tension. There had been too many long days in a row, she realized. There had been no more kisses, and she had told herself that was for the best even as she felt the dull ache of disappointment. Reminded herself of it even as she caught herself staring at his perfect lips in meetings or when they met in his office or hers about the renovations.

Once she walked in while he had Gina on speakerphone. She'd paused, unsure of what to do, but Luca had waved her in. His hair stood up in rows where his fingers had run through it and the scowl line was back between his brows. They were speaking in Italian, but at the end, his voice softened. "I love you, Gigi. *Ciao*."

The line was disconnected.

"You're worried about her. Is everything okay?"

His smile was thin. "It will be. She says hello, by the way."

Their obvious closeness made her wish once more for the family she'd never had. Seeing Luca with his sister, teasing, arguing, and like today—always supportive—made her long for it.

For the first time, she felt free to be herself. Luca

had no expectations of her and that was liberating. The way he smiled seemed as if it were just for her. The way he'd held her hand felt like it had always been that way. And his kisses had taken her breath away. Even knowing it was imprudent, she couldn't help but wish he'd do it again.

The clincher had been when the delivery man had arrived on Saturday morning.

She'd carefully unwrapped the package, staring down at the painting she'd admired during their trip to the gallery. The fact that he had spent so much money to buy it and give it to her said it all. It didn't require a note, but there was a brief one anyway, scrawled on a plain white card…

When it speaks to your heart, you know it's the right one.

No one had ever given her such a gift. And it wasn't the money. She knew now that the price tag meant nothing to Luca. And it hadn't been for appearances; if he'd wanted to impress he would have given her jewelry. This was more personal. It was perfect.

She had yet to thank him, though. Saturday had rolled into Sunday and she'd spent the day cleaning and picking up groceries…she hadn't noticed the fridge, but she had noticed Tommy's empty food bowl. Now it was Monday and the opportunity hadn't arisen.

She wasn't sure what she'd say. She'd glimpsed him this morning, walking through the lobby and her heart had given a little leap just at the sight of him. She was falling for him. She hadn't wanted a relationship and even now it wasn't a real one, but she couldn't help her feelings. She saw so many things in Luca to love. She knew now she'd seen them in the beginning, but hadn't recognized them as they'd been blanketed in her own fears and in-securities. The truth was, he was a conscientious, caring boss who worked hard and was extremely capable. Luca wasn't the irresponsible playboy she'd expected. He was nothing like.

If she thanked him for the painting now, she'd probably make a complete fool of herself and say something sentimental.

She had to keep her head. Soon Luca would be gone. She'd get over her feelings. She'd be fine. She'd look back on it all as a beautiful time.

Mari stepped into the lobby, her eyes taking in the changes that were ongoing. The lobby was, for all intents and purposes, operating in half its usual square footage while the other half underwent its transformation. Even though they'd cordoned off the area being worked on, there was still mess and disorder, and she wondered if it would have been better to close the hotel for a few months. On the other hand…she looked at the staff. They were doing a fantastic job of adjusting. More than one had mentioned to her how excited they were to be able to take part in it all. And while she'd felt duty-bound to try to keep a check on the plans, she could admit to herself that Luca had been right. He *was* good at his job. The hotel was going to be stunning when it was completed.

But as she turned, she caught sight of a man at the makeshift reception desk. Something about him unnerved Mari. She couldn't pinpoint it, but a cold feeling of uneasiness swept through her. Colleen, the employee behind the desk, had a smile pasted on her face but Mari could tell it was forced. The man gestured with his hands and Mari heard his raised voice carry across the lobby, over the construction noise.

But it was her job to deal with this sort of thing, no matter how distasteful. She gave her shoulders one last roll, put on her friendliest smile and went forward.

"Good afternoon, and welcome to the Fiori Cascade. Is there some way I can be of assistance?"

Colleen's taut cheeks relaxed a bit. "Good afternoon, Ms. Ross. I was just explaining to Mr. Reilly that we've adjusted his reservation to a room on the third floor. Due to the renovations."

Mr. Reilly was not appeased. "And I was telling *her*—" he turned his back on Colleen altogether "—that arrangement is completely unacceptable."

Mari clenched her teeth. He had presented his back to Colleen, the slight deliberate and rude. But he was their guest and he had been inconvenienced.

It was her job to smooth ruffled feathers. "I'm the manager here, perhaps I can be of help. You were booked in which room?"

"The Primrose," Colleen supplied over his shoulder.

Mari kept the warm smile in place. The Primrose Room was one of their best, and it was also nonexistent now. "I'm afraid the room you originally booked is now involved in extensive renovations. To compensate you, Mr. Reilly, we can accommodate you in a third floor executive suite at no additional cost. I'm sure you'll find the room more than satisfactory. Our executive suites feature a generously sized—"

"I reserved this room three months ago and it's the room I'll have," he interrupted sharply. "I don't want a suite on the third floor. I want the Primrose."

Mari breathed in measured breaths. Everything about Reilly was pushing her buttons, from his rudeness to his sense of obligation to the belligerent tone of voice.

"And I'm very sorry it's impossible, as the room is part of our upgrading." She tried a smile, hoping to appeal to his common sense. "Presently the room is full of plywood and power tools. As manager here, I do apologize on behalf of the hotel and will be more than happy to move you to the suite and also include breakfast each morning. I assure you, Mr. Reilly, our executive suites are beyond compare." Her voice came out warm and confident, but inside she was trembling, hating the confrontation.

She tried to remember the exercises her therapist had taught her. It went against everything she'd learned growing up. That to stay silent meant to stay safe. It was her job to talk to him. Yet for a moment she became the girl huddled in a corner hoping to be left alone.

She looked over his shoulder at Colleen. "You'll see to it, Colleen?"

"Yes, Ms. Ross."

Mari aimed a parting smile at him and took two steps away.

"If you think that's good enough, you're mistaken, missy. Don't you walk away from me!"

A heavy hand reached out and gripped her wrist painfully, jerking her back and she yelped and cowered before she could think better of it. Her eyes closed, waiting for what would come next, the sound of Colleen's shocked gasp vibrating through her. She stilled. It was only worse when she showed pain or fear.

"Is there a problem here?"

Mari gazed up at Luca, wanting to weep with gratitude. Luca, eyes dark with fury, glared like an avenging angel at the man holding her arm. She'd never been so glad to see someone in all her life.

"Nothing I can't handle," the man sneered, giving her wrist an extra squeeze. Mari couldn't help the wince that flickered over her face, and instantly saw a muscle in Luca's jaw twitch in response.

"I strongly suggest you release the lady's arm." He uttered the words softly but the steely threat was unmistakable. When Reilly didn't immediately comply, Luca's voice was dangerously low. "While you still can."

"We were just having a little disagreement, that's all," the man replied, looking disappointed at having to relinquish his hold on Mari. Now that her wrist was free, she rubbed it with her hand. She knew she should say something, but words refused to come. She stood dumbly, staring at Luca.

"Mari, are you all right?" He temporarily took his eyes off the man, the look of genuine concern reaching through the fear and touching her deep inside. Luca wouldn't let anything happen to her. She nodded slightly and forced calm breaths. All she wanted was for Reilly to leave. To get him out of her sight.

"Perhaps I may be of some assistance," Luca suggested tightly, his polite words laced with venom. Mari held her breath, hoping Luca didn't resort to violence. Causing a scene was clearly what the man wanted. A chill ran over her body. She knew his kind. The kind that wanted to provoke a fight. Who thought physical power solved everything.

"And who might you be?"

"Luca Fiori. Owner of this hotel."

The man smiled suddenly. "Mr. Fiori. I think perhaps you need to teach your staff the principle of the customer is always right. I booked the Primrose Room months ago, and now I'm being put in some third-rate room."

Mari spoke for the first time. She lifted her chin and willed her voice to come out without the wobble she felt inside. "I moved Mr. Reilly to the suites on the third floor."

"The Fiori Cascade is very sorry for the inconvenience, as I'm sure our manager, Ms. Ross, communicated to you." Reilly started to open his mouth but Luca cut him off. "However, we do not tolerate abuse of any kind toward our staff. She has generously booked you in one of our most exclusive suites. I'm sure you'll find it more than satisfactory."

"I assure you I won't." He turned his head and glared at Mari.

Mari dropped her gaze to the floor. She didn't want to challenge him in any way. Luca was letting him stay. It was smart businesswise, but she couldn't help being disappointed. She refused to look up. If he had to think he'd won, fine. It was better than the alternative.

Luca saw Mari's gaze drop and stay focused on the floor. She was still afraid. For the tiniest flash, he remembered her vibrancy, her laughter, on the night that they danced together. No man—client or not—had the right to frighten her, to intimidate her. To use force against her. He held his temper, but only just.

"Come to think of it, Mr. Reilly, we're terribly sorry but the Cascade has no vacancies at this time. I'm certain you'll be able to find lodging at one of Banff's other fine establishments. Please leave."

"Like hell! I intend to let head office know of this!"

His attempts to defuse the situation had failed and Luca knew that he couldn't have such a person staying at the hotel under any circumstances. This scene had to end and end now. If Reilly would do this in a public lobby, what would happen if housekeeping upset him in some way? He had a duty to protect his staff. He had a duty to Mari. Luca knew Reilly would follow through and lodge a complaint, even if it meant he would only make a fool of himself.

"Please do. I'm sure my assistant will forward your complaint to me with the utmost expediency."

"You bast…"

Luca interrupted, any pretence of amicability gone. His words were clipped and final. "I am sure the local authorities would be happy to provide transportation, if you can't leave under your own power." Luca flicked a finger by his thigh, knowing two of the hotel security would join them within seconds. He would have preferred not to get police involved, but there was a limit and Mr. Reilly had crossed it.

Reilly squared his shoulders, gathered his bags and strode out of the lobby, cursing the whole way.

Mari looked up at him, her cheeks still devoid of healthy color. "I'm sorry, Luca, I didn't mean to…"

"Don't apologize. Come with me."

She followed meekly. He didn't touch her anywhere but she felt pulled along just the same. "Where are we going?"

"To my suite, so you can get yourself together."

He opened the door with his key and she went inside ahead of him. He went to the cabinet and poured a small amount of brandy in a glass. He handed it to her. "Drink this. It will put the color back in your cheeks."

Mari sipped, opening her mouth wide and gasping as the liquor burned.

He was angry. She'd handled everything wrong and he was angry at her. At least he was going to have the grace to discuss it in private.

"Luca, I'm sorry." She took another fortifying sip of the brandy and handed him back the glass.

"Sorry for what?"

"It's my job to deal with our guests and I failed today."

"For God's sake, quit apologizing for that ape's behavior!"

She stepped back at his outburst.

He tempered his tone at her reaction. "I'm the one that's sorry, Mariella. When I saw him grab you…you looked like you were about to collapse in a heap. It made me insensible."

"You're not angry with me?"

He stepped forward and crushed her into his arms. "No, darling," he whispered into her ear. "I'm not angry."

Tears stung the backs of her eyelids as they slid closed. His wide hand cradled the back of her head as she leaned against him.

"I saw him touch you and I wanted to grab him by the neck and throw him out," Luca ground out beside her ear. "But that's not Fiori. At least that's not what the hotel stands for. Fiori is class and elegance, not brawling in the lobby. Even if he deserved it."

"I'm glad you didn't. I...I hate violence. But I was afraid, Luca. So afraid."

"It took all I had to hold my temper."

She stepped back out of his arms. "You may think you were polite, but I saw the look of thunder on your face. Oh, Luca, I was so glad to see you. I knew you wouldn't let anything happen to me."

He lifted a finger and ran it over her cheek. "I'd never let him hurt you, Mariella."

"But I know...I know what men like Reilly can do."

And then the shakes hit.

Mari felt the trembling strike deep inside and was helpless to control it. Her body went cold and suddenly it was impossible to get enough air. She stared straight ahead but could hear the gasping of her own strident breath.

"Porco mondo!" Mari barely registered Luca's exclamation as his hands gripped her arms and pushed her down on the sofa. He said something to her in fast Italian. The breaths came fast and shallow and she started to see gray spots.

"Damn it! Mari, put your head between your legs!" He bit out the command and she felt the pressure of his hand against her head, pushing it down. She closed her eyes and fought against the darkness. "Breathe, darling," his voice came, gentler now, and she concentrated simply on the in and out of respiration.

Reilly was gone. Robert was gone. No one would hurt her.

If she said it over enough, perhaps she'd believe it.

After a few minutes she'd gained control again. The shakes had hit her so hard and fast she hadn't been prepared, though she should have been. She'd had them often enough before. It just hadn't happened for a very long time. She'd let her guard down since being with Luca day in and day out. She was safe here with him. He was looking after her and knowing it made her want to cry all over again. She was always alone. This time she wasn't. Luca was here.

"You… I thought you were going to hit him," she murmured, bracing her arms on her knees and holding her head.

"And I wanted to, the moment I saw him put his hand on you. But sometimes there are better ways to accomplish things than with fists. He's gone now, and he won't be back. Not to any Fiori hotel. I'll make sure of it."

At his words a tear snuck out of the corner of her eye and she blotted it. He couldn't know how much his words meant to her. How much he'd risen in her eyes, just knowing he'd preferred a calmer, more effective way to deal with a brute. Knowing he had had that urge to protect her, yet controlled his temper.

The warmth of his body disappeared for a moment and she heard him over at the bar. When he came back he pressed a glass of water into her hands. "This might work better than the brandy," he suggested quietly, his fingers cupping hers around the glass.

She took a grateful sip. Wondered what she could possibly say to make him understand. Understand both why she'd reacted the way she had and also understand how much it meant to her, having him there with her.

"Mariella, is there anything you could have done to make Reilly happy?"

She took another sip. "Short of magically making the Primrose Room appear out of our new massage facility, I doubt it. But I should have found a way. We were the ones who inconvenienced him. I should have found a better way. He was within his rights to be angry…"

"Don't you dare make excuses. Don't you dare, Mariella. There is no excuse for a man raising his hand to a woman. Ever."

In the moment when Reilly had grabbed her arm, she had forgotten everything she'd learned since that day seven years ago. She'd forgotten how to be right and instead had only known what it was to feel wrong. And Luca was right. She was making excuses. She'd been good at it. Good at blaming herself, at playing the "if only" game. If only she'd been smarter, prettier, better behaved. If only she'd said something different, or nothing at all. If she hadn't looked into his eyes, if she'd cooked the pasta a few minutes longer, if only, if only, if only.

And for a few seconds, she'd truly believed, if only she had looked away, said something differently, maybe Mr. Reilly wouldn't have grabbed her. Seven years of progress down the drain.

"Mariella." Luca knelt by her knees. "Sweetheart. I saw your face when he put his hands on you. You went so pale. That's happened to you before, hasn't it."

She would not cry. She would not.

She nodded, a tiny affirmation.

"Oh, Mariella, I am so sorry."

This kinder, gentler Luca was tearing her defenses apart bit by bit. Every place his hand touched was warmed and reassured. Every word he said healed something inside her. She didn't want his pity. All she wanted was his understanding and…and…

And his love. It was all she'd ever really wanted and she hadn't even known it.

Luca continued on. "It all makes sense now. That day in the attic, all those times you didn't want to be touched. Who was he, Mariella? An ex-husband?"

She shook her head.

"A boyfriend then."

Mari shook her head again. "No, nothing like that." She could trust Luca, she knew that in her heart. They could deny their feelings all they wanted, but the way he'd rushed to her rescue proved it. He had earned the right to the truth. To know why she'd acted the way she had all these weeks. "It was my stepfather."

Luca said a word in Italian she didn't understand but the meaning was clear enough. "He beat you?"

"Yes. Me and…and my mother."

Luca stood, went to the bar, poured himself a drink far more generous than the one he'd given her and tossed it back.

"And where is he now?"

Mari folded her hands in her lap. It helped with the trembling. She tried not to think about the beatings. About how Robert would turn to her after he'd gotten tired of pushing her mother around. "He…he was in jail, but he's out now. He made parole the day before you and I went…" She had to stop, breathe, swallow. "The day in the attic."

"Why didn't you tell me before?"

She looked up from her lap then. What she saw in Luca's eyes she knew she'd remember to her dying day. He wasn't angry with her, he was angry *for* her. Ready to stand between her and whoever would dare to hurt her.

"He's on parole, you said. Would he come after you? Damn it, Mari, I could have protected you! You should have said something, rather than go through this alone!"

"What would I have said, Luca?"

He put down his glass. "If I had known you were scared, if I'd known the reason you didn't like contact, I swear Mari, I wouldn't have pushed. I'm not cruel."

"And said what? 'Hey, Mr. New Boss! Please don't mind me, I just don't like any physical contact because my stepfather was a sadistic freak that beat me for the hell of it?' Nice ice breaker, don't you think?"

His eyes closed for the smallest of moments.

"All the times I held you, all the times I could feel you trembling. *Dio,* Mari, I'm so sorry."

He was blaming himself now and Mari was sick and tired of Robert Langston having all the power. Could she be honest with Luca? Could she tell him how she felt?

In the end she knew she couldn't reveal it all, yet she also felt he deserved a partial truth.

"I wasn't shaking with fear, Luca. Not with you. Don't you realize how much it means to me that you stood up for me today? No one's ever done that for me before. I…I…" But she stopped. She couldn't tell him how she felt, it was too new, too tenuous. "Please, don't ever think I was afraid of you. I *never* felt like I was in physical danger."

Only in danger of what I feel for you, she thought. That was the part she couldn't tell him. That was the one thing she couldn't let him know. She had known from the beginning that there would never be anything serious between them. He was Luca Fiori, based in Florence, heir to the empire. They were from two different worlds and were simply in the same place at a particular time.

He couldn't know that with each passing day, with each gesture, she was falling deeper in love with him. What was she to do with those feelings? She certainly didn't feel equipped to handle them, let alone share them. The one thing that she was sure of was that it wouldn't turn out well. And she valued him too much to let things turn bitter and angry.

"Are you afraid now? Of your stepfather? What about your mother? Where is she?"

She wasn't sure how much to tell him, how much he could handle. It wasn't a pretty story. She paused too long and he backed away.

"I apologize. I've overstepped. You don't want to talk about it, and I respect that."

"No!" Mari got up from the sofa. "I'm not trying to shut you out, Luca…you must understand. No one here knows about this. I started a new life, built it from scratch. And I thought I'd left it all behind me. I did therapy. I thought it was all okay. Only I have just realized I can't leave it behind—Reilly showed me that—and right now…"

She needed him. Luca, complicated, arrogant, and temporary—wasn't that a kick in the pants.

"Right now—" her voice shook "—you're the only one keeping me from losing it. Today brought it all back, all of it. I…I need you, Luca."

She half expected him to run screaming. What man would want an emotionally crippled woman clinging and crying all over him?

"Tell me," he said softly, holding out his hand.

She took it. "Robert Langston spent seven years in prison for the attempted murder of my mother… and of me."

CHAPTER NINE

LUCA sat beside her on the plush sofa, tucking one leg beneath him so that he was sitting sideways, facing her. His warm hand enclosed hers and she clung to the thought of it, a link that kept her from feeling groundless and out of control. Now that she said the words they sounded surreal. Like it couldn't have possibly happened. But it had, and she squeezed his hand in response.

She didn't talk about that day. Not ever. But perhaps now she needed to. This afternoon had taught her that it wasn't behind her as she'd thought it was. And the scary truth was Robert *was* out of prison and knowing it had chipped away at her safety barrier more than she cared to admit. Being with Luca was the only thing holding her together right now.

She looked up at him. His dark eyes were steady on hers, waiting for her to begin, giving her the time she needed. There was such a strength about him, even now when he was being gentle and nurturing. Luca was a man to be relied upon, so much more than the media's Fiori heir who liked fast cars and beautiful women. That wasn't the real Luca.

The real Luca was sitting before her now, a safe port in the storm, willing to be whatever she needed.

She stared at the sensuous curve of his lips, feeling a little wonder that a man like him had kissed a woman like her, and on more than one occasion. Things like that didn't happen. Real life wasn't like that.

They certainly didn't happen to a plain Jane from Ontario. Not one who was mediocre at best. But here he was, waiting. Not running. Not arguing. He was caring for her, and knowing it unlocked something she kept hidden deep inside. For the first time in her life, she wanted to *give* of herself to another human being.

"Mariella, you don't have to tell me if it's too difficult. It's okay."

She was brought back by the warm sound of his voice. She lifted their joined hands and kissed the top of his, holding it against her lips. She closed her eyes, grateful he was there. Even now he was being understanding and her appreciation ran long and deep. When she was with him, Robert somehow lost his power.

"When I was six, my mother married Robert Langston." She focused on Luca's face to keep the images away. "I never knew my real father. She'd brought me up on her own all that time and she said that things would get better, we'd have a new family. Only it didn't turn out that way."

"It wasn't the fairy tale you expected."

She nodded. "The abuse didn't happen right at the beginning, but that doesn't matter now. What is important is that when it did start it escalated quickly and completely, and we were essentially terrorized. He had complete control. He ruled us with fear, and it was awful. The years were…"

But she couldn't go on. Her throat closed over as memories flooded back; cowering in a corner while he yelled at her mother. The rage on his face as he used his fists on her. Mari had foolishly spent too many evenings trying to defend her mother, only to receive the same treatment.

The years of long-sleeved shirts and makeup. Being scared to speak up and feeling guilty listening to the sound of punches on the other side of the wall, too paralyzed to do anything. Of tiptoeing around, always afraid of saying the wrong thing or doing something not quite the right way.

Years of waiting for her mother to tell her it was over, but that moment never came. She'd remained trapped in the living hell of her childhood.

For the first time, Mari forgot all the police reports, all the therapy, all the ways she'd been told she'd made progress, and she simply cried—quiet, cold, devastating tears.

Luca pulled her into his arms and held her… warm, solid, sure. She cried for the childhood she'd lost, the guilt she still felt, the fear that never quite went away, and the fact that today of all days it had finally reached the point where she could grieve for it all.

Luca had made that possible. By some miracle, he'd pushed himself into her life and had shown her what was real.

After several minutes she slid backward on the couch, wiping her eyes. Luca went to the bathroom and brought back a box of tissues, offering her two and waiting patiently.

"I'm sorry for crying all over you that way."

"Please don't apologize." He sat on the edge of the coffee table, facing her. "I just want to make sure you're all right."

At that moment the telephone rang and Luca scowled. "Answer it," Mari said, but Luca shook his head.

"It can wait."

The ringing persisted and he sighed, rising to answer. Mari watched him from her position on the couch. She was tired, so tired. Only once before had she been this drained, and it was the day she'd had to testify in court.

"It will have to wait."

Mari heard Luca speaking into the telephone. His eyes remained fixed on her and she tried tucking the hair that had come loose back behind her ears. She must look a fright. His voice came again. "I'm sorry, but I'm in the middle of something more important right now. You'll have to take care of it. I'll call you tomorrow."

He hung up the phone and came back, sitting on the table again and taking her hands in his. "I'm sorry about that."

She was still trying to absorb the fact that he'd put off whoever it was to look after her. "If you need to go, it's fine. I'll be okay."

"You're not okay. And it can wait. Right now looking after you is my priority."

Never, not once in her life had anyone said those words to her. Never had anyone put her first. But Luca—driven, workaholic Luca—had just put off whoever had been on the other end of that call. She licked her lips, unsure of where to start.

"Today I forgot all the things I learned from counseling and only felt the fear, the responsibility. If only I'd done something differently it wouldn't have happened. I…" She swallowed, having difficulty going on. "Oh, Luca, I thought I was far beyond that. I worked so hard and all of a sudden it was like no time had passed at all. And then you were there. I was so glad to see you."

"He put his hands on you. I couldn't allow that." He lifted his other hand and grazed her cheek with his fingers.

"In that moment I was trapped, back seven years ago. That day…" Her voice faded away for a moment. It was all in the police report. It was in her medical files after she'd gone through intensive counseling. But she'd never willingly offered it to someone who hadn't been paid to hear it.

"What happened that day, Mariella?"

His voice encouraged her, invited her. After all he'd done, telling him seemed the next logical, if difficult step.

"I had moved out, and felt torn because on one hand I had left my mum behind. On the other I was away and safe. Mum had called and had said she was finally leaving him." Mari realized her eyes were bone-dry; she must have cried herself out earlier. She remembered being so relieved, so happy that her mum was getting away. Happy at the thought that maybe, just maybe, they could start building a relationship. "I said I'd come and help. But when I arrived, he'd gotten there first. Caught her packing her bags and when I found her she was bleeding, unconscious on the floor, with a broken arm and a cracked skull. Her clothes were strewn everywhere, slashed to ribbons."

"*Dio Mio.*" Luca's low exclamation drew her out of the memory.

"It happens, Luca, far more often than it should."

She put her other hand over his. Telling him was sapping her strength but it needed to be said. Perhaps she could finally be free of it. Perhaps with Luca beside her, she'd stop blaming herself. Perhaps Robert would lose his power over her for good.

"He found me there, grabbing the phone to call the police. He ripped it from my hand and started in on me. By the time it was over, my mum was still unconscious and I had a concussion, broken ribs and internal injuries from where he—" Her voice broke a little. "From where he kicked me over and over. He left us there, Luca. Left us to die. But the postman noticed bloody handprints on the front door and the stair railing. He called the police and the rest is history."

"Only it's not history." He gently tipped up her chin with a finger. "Nothing like that can ever completely go away, can it. Oh, Mari." He lifted her hands to his lips and kissed the backs, his eyes closing. She stared at the way his lashes lay on his cheeks, the tender way he cradled her fingers. Where had he come from? How was it that he was here, exactly what she needed, at exactly the time she needed him?

"I am so sorry. No one should ever go through something like that." He whispered the words against her fingertips.

And then he leaned forward and touched his lips to hers.

She went into his embrace willingly, their knees pressed together between the sofa and table. He was strong, and somehow a barrier between her and the ugliness of her past. When she was with him she was the Mariella she'd always wanted to be, free of the hold Robert Langston had held over her for so many years.

The kiss was soft, tentative, sweet. She hadn't known he was capable of sweet.

She hadn't known she was capable of love, but here it was. She loved Luca. And being completely out of her depth, she had no idea what to do about it.

"And now he's out of prison…are you afraid he'll come after you? What about your mum?"

His voice drew her back into the present. "The authorities keep me up-to-date while he's on probation. Of course I think of it, and wonder if he hates me for my part in sending him to jail. But I can't let myself think of it too much or it becomes overwhelming. I spent too many years looking over my shoulder. And it's not one of those things you ever really get used to."

"And what about your mother?"

Mari shook her head. "I don't speak to my mum that often… there seems to be a wall between us now. I don't even know where she's living. I…" Mari cleared her throat. "A part of me still wonders how she could have let it happen. How she could have stayed with a man who beat her. Who beat me. Why didn't she try to get out?"

She looked up at Luca. "What kind of mother hurts her own child that way? What kind of mother doesn't put the welfare of her child ahead of everything? There have been times I've thought about the home I want, the children I might have someday. Could I put them through that? I know I couldn't. I've tried to understand it, but I just can't. The only thing I can come up with is that she was too afraid to do anything else."

Luca shook his head. "I don't know, either. I barely remember my mother myself."

"You said she left you and Gina. That must have been difficult."

"I only remember feeling like we never mattered." Mari's eyes widened at the loathing in his tone. "She left us when I was a boy. My dad raised Gina and me."

He stood up and walked over to the window.

"I'm sorry," she murmured, "That must have been horrible for you. Did your dad ever remarry?"

He cleared his throat. "It's not important, Mari. It was a long time ago. And it was nothing compared to what you went through. Nothing."

He spoke with such vehemence that she knew he was hiding his own hurts.

And for a moment, she forgot about herself and wondered about the boy he'd been, and how he'd suffered in his own way. Perhaps that silver spoon he'd been born with didn't gleam as brightly as she'd thought. How she wished she could help him as he'd helped her today.

How had this happened?

She'd fallen in love with Luca Fiori, and it was the one sure thing to break her heart. Luca cared for her, yes. She knew that. But love? By his own admission, Luca didn't *do* love.

She had to take a step back. This baring of souls—well hers, anyway—was all well and good, but even she wasn't fool enough to believe there was a happy ending in all of it. Luca didn't live here. He didn't belong here. He belonged at his villa in Italy with his family and the Fiori empire and what was happening between them now was a blip in their lives. Necessary, perhaps, but still temporary. How could she tell him her true feelings?

She stared at his back, trying to puzzle it out but not getting very far. Perhaps she was just raw from everything that had happened. What if these feelings were just a byproduct of a process she should have gone through years ago? It would be foolish to make this into more than it was, and Mari was smart enough to know her perspective was skewed.

"You're categorizing."

Luca's voice reached her. He hadn't turned back around, but stared out into the growing darkness.

"I can practically hear your mind working, Mari. Please don't. Just let things be."

Mari rose and went to the window, standing behind him. She wasn't sure anything would be the right move, so she simply did what she felt like: she put her arms around his body and pressed her cheek into the warmth of his back.

* * *

Luca swallowed against the lump that had formed in his throat. Anything he'd gone through as a child was nothing, nothing compared to the hell that Mari had experienced. He tried to picture her on a floor, battered and bruised, and couldn't. It seemed too wrong, too horrific. What sort of man did that to another human being? To a woman he was supposed to love?

And yet, here she was, somehow comforting him.

"It's snowing," he murmured. Soft flakes fluttered past the balcony railing, settling on the ground in intricate patterns. He was reminded of his grandmother's lace and wondered what she'd think of this mess he'd got himself into.

Why was it that people hurt the ones they were supposed to love? He knew he couldn't let Mari do this alone, yet it brought back memories he hated, ones of comforting Gina when their mother had abandoned the family. *Nonna* had always been there to help. What would she say now, if she could be here?

He knew exactly what she'd say and he didn't like the answer. She'd tell him to stop holding a grudge and forgive.

Mari sighed against his back and he closed his eyes. What a day they'd had. He was glad now that he had handled Reilly the way he had. If this was what Mari was carrying deep inside, a physical response would have only frightened her more.

Today he'd thought only of Mari. And that wasn't good.

Mari did not need a man like him. She needed someone she could rely on. Someone who could give her stability and security and make a home with her. She'd even mentioned it, the longing for a home and children. That wasn't his life, it never had been. He'd always been the Fiori heir, the one everyone assumed would step into his father's shoes one day. And he kept fighting against it.

He looked at the reflection of the suite in the glass doors. There was nothing personal here, no pictures, no trinkets, nothing to make it a home and that was how he lived his life. It was what it was. It was the world he inhabited.

He'd forget about her, eventually.

But with her arms around him, the only thing he wanted to do was lift her in his arms and hold on.

And he'd come as close to admitting his feelings as he ever would.

"Stay tonight, Mari."

Her head lifted from his back and it felt cold where it had been warm a second ago.

"Luca, I…"

"Not in my bed." For once in his life this had nothing to do with sex. He turned, wanting her to understand how he couldn't say the words. "Just…stay. I'd only worry about you if you went home. You can have the bed. I'll sleep on the sofa."

"What you did for me today, Luca, no one's ever done anything like that for me before. I can't impose on you further."

"You're not imposing."

For a long moment their gazes clung. Words hung unspoken.

"Wait here."

He disappeared into the bedroom and returned with a T-shirt. "I don't have pyjamas to lend you."

She took the T-shirt. "Thank you."

She disappeared into his room, and he heard the bathroom door shut behind her. When he didn't hear anything after several minutes, he decided he should check on her.

She was in his bed, the duvet pulled up to her chin. Her blotchy cheeks were relaxed and her eyelashes were smudges against her cheeks. She'd fallen asleep before he could even ask if she was hungry.

He'd let her sleep. And when she woke he'd make sure she was all right.

And then, somehow, he'd find a way out of this mess.

Mari woke to sunlight filtering through the bedroom window. Pushing her hair out of her face, she realized she was in Luca's bed, the smell of his cosmetics faint in the sheets and sounds of him tinkering in the suite filtering through.

She'd spent the night. And she hadn't given a

thought to going home or to Tommy…she could only hope he'd used the dog door on the porch.

Mari checked her watch: 9:00 a.m. Oh my God. She'd slept straight through, with none of the nightmares that had haunted her lately. Any lingering thoughts were crowded out by the knowledge that full-day staff were in the hotel and she only had yesterday's clothes to dress in. She should have used her head last night.

But nothing about yesterday had been about logic or sense.

"Good morning," Luca said from the doorway to the bedroom.

She scrambled up to a seated position. "Luca, I'm so sorry. I slept…"

"Here all night," he finished, a smile on his lips. His elbow leaned casually against the door frame. "Slept nearly fifteen hours."

"I must have been more tired than I realized." He was acting like this was normal, for Pete's sake! And seeing him brought back everything that had happened yesterday with a vengeance. Including kissing him, crying on him, realizing she loved him…

And in the silence she felt a blush creep up her neck and bloom in her cheeks. Somehow she had to get out of this situation with a modicum of grace. In the bright light of day it was clearer than ever that revealing her true feelings would be a mistake. She just needed time to figure out exactly what was what.

"I think that sleep might have been a long time coming," he replied lazily.

A knock sounded at the door. Mari lifted her eyebrows in his direction. He merely shrugged.

"You grew restless a while ago. I ordered up breakfast. You must be starving…you didn't have any dinner."

He opened the door while Mari hastily pulled on her clothes, jamming her hair back into the clip she'd worn yesterday. As she came out of the bedroom, one of their staff wheeled in a cart adorned with silver domed trays.

"Thank you, Geoff." Luca handed a bill to the server who nodded, then smiled in Mari's direction.

Mari frowned as the door shut with a quiet click. "I don't want this getting around the staff. What are they going to think of me up here in your suite?"

"You've been here before."

"Not looking like this. Not coming out of your bedroom."

Luca moved the cart closer to the dining table. "Don't worry, I'm used to it. It always blows over."

Mari's mouth clamped shut. Luca was used to these situations. She was not. If he was trying to put the morning in perspective, he was doing a stand-up job.

"I'm sorry about yesterday. I shouldn't have unloaded on you." She felt obligated to apologize.

Suddenly there seemed to be a new awkwardness between them. Now that it was over and done with, perhaps he was feeling embarrassed at being privy to all her secrets. She couldn't say she blamed him.

A shadow crossed his features.

"It's fine. It's good that you did. I imagine it feels better to have it out. I understand, Mari, I really do."

Why was he acting so differently? Yesterday he'd held her hand and she'd told him her deepest troubles. He'd leaped to her defense and he'd held her in his arms as she'd cried. Now… God, now he was treating her like she was one of his flings. One of the women he kept on his arm.

Her mouth soured. She'd thought she'd been right to put her trust in him, but his casual treatment of her this morning was a letdown. She'd wanted to mean more to him. Which was silly because she already knew in her heart they had no future. He'd come right out and said so. He didn't do *love*.

"Come, eat. You must be starving."

"I need to go home and change." Mari stood and smoothed her slacks.

"There's no need. I had some things sent up from the boutique. You're welcome to use the shower here."

Mari gritted her teeth.

He was treating her like…like nothing monumental had ever happened between them! He was taking charge and deciding what she'd do and when. And damn it, she was done being on anyone's timetable!

He lifted the lid on a platter. The smell of French toast reached her nostrils, the tantalizing scent of vanilla and cinnamon and maple. Her stomach growled. In all the uproar, she hadn't eaten last night. It would serve him right if she sat and ate the whole serving!

"I would have thought that privilege was one reserved for your affairs," she remarked caustically, putting her hands in her pockets and clenching her fingers tightly.

She'd told him everything last night, everything about Robert and her fears and today he treated her as a polite stranger. There was only one explanation.

It had been too much. Her baggage was too much for him and it had been foolish to think that Luca could handle it. As much as she'd wanted to believe in him, she'd expected far more than he could give. She wasn't sophisticated and uncomplicated. She was a mess and he was politely backing away.

She could hardly hate him for it. Even if his cool treatment of her this morning stung. She longed to simply flee, but somehow she knew she had to handle this with some sort of dignity and composure. It would only be more awkward later if she ran out. They still had to work together for the time remaining in the renovations.

* * *

Luca ignored the voice inside that told him to knock it off. He looked at Mari and could only see her face last night as she told him about her stepfather. He'd had to help her. He'd wanted to.

But now, in the bright light of day, he needed to step back. This felt too much like a relationship and he wasn't prepared. The last time he'd been involved with a woman deeper than a dating level, he'd let it interfere with work, too. He'd fallen for Ellie, had trusted her. He'd told her that he loved her. Only that time he'd discovered it wasn't him she wanted at all, but his Fiori connection. The Fiori name almost seemed a curse to love, and he wasn't willing to put his heart out there again.

So these feelings for Mari weren't supposed to have happened at all. Their kisses shouldn't have happened. His eyes remained cool even though he knew she was right. This was exactly what he would have done for a woman the morning after, and the truth of it stung. "That's a bit low."

"I'm sorry, Luca. I think I'm still a little off balance after yesterday. I believe I will eat something," she said, going to the dining table and taking a seat. A platter glistened with raisin-studded French toast and fragrant circles of ham. She filled a plate and poured warm maple syrup over the lot of it.

He should have known better than to flirt with her like he did with other women. Mari wasn't that type and somehow he needed to extricate himself from whatever it was they shared. But he would not call it a relationship. In relationships people hurt each other. Like his father had been hurt. Like he'd been hurt when Ellie betrayed him. He'd told Ellie things and she'd used them to hurt him later, to taunt him.

Mari wouldn't do that, the voice inside argued. But this time that wasn't his worry. He was more worried *he'd* hurt *her,* and she'd been hurt enough. What an unusual position he found himself in.

A break to friendship was the best plan, wasn't it? Mari didn't need a man who would break her heart. And a man who didn't *do* relationships surely would. What she needed now was a friend.

"Juice, freshly squeezed." Solicitously he poured her a generous glass. "Enough vitamin C to last all day."

"Thank you." She sipped, then put the glass down and picked up her fork. "Aren't you going to eat anything?"

"Indeed."

He took the seat opposite and uncovered another platter containing scrambled eggs and a bowl of mixed berries.

Mari took one bite, then two, wondering how long she could be expected to survive this agony. Eating breakfast like there was nothing to be said. It was a complete farce after their intimacy of the day before. There was nothing to fault in his behavior.

Nothing. It was perfectly polite. But it was clear he was distancing himself.

It was cold as hell.

She wanted to ask him, didn't yesterday mean anything to you? Wanted to say how much she appreciated how he'd taken care of her. But she couldn't. He was acting like it had meant nothing. Like having breakfast together in his suite was an ordinary occurrence. It was no more personal than…than a business meeting.

The bite she was chewing went down with difficulty. There was only so long she could keep this up. She was still raw from yesterday's events and the insight that she'd fallen for Luca. For him to treat her so now was confusing and insulting and it hurt. Made her wonder if she'd imagined his gentle understanding all along. If he'd only been placating her because she'd been so distraught.

She put down her fork, keeping her mask carefully in place. She had misjudged him, had misplaced her trust. It just went to prove how poor her judgment still was.

"Thank you for breakfast, but I need to go now."

She pushed out her chair, avoiding his gaze.

"There's no need. You can refresh yourself here, Mariella. I'm sure the clothes I sent for will fit. You can go straight to your office from here."

Oh, he had it all planned out. He'd had lots of time to think about it, all evening last night while she'd slept, no doubt. His consideration was hardly touching. Nothing he could have said or done this morning could have made her feel worse than this politeness.

"You have it all planned out, don't you Luca?" She struggled to keep the tremble out of her voice. "I thought I was the one for planning and you were the impulsive one, but how wrong I was. You've planned it from the beginning—how to get around the difficult manager, how to handle your sister, how to handle me."

He put down the spoon of berries he was holding. "I'm sorry?"

Mari straightened her blouse and looked around to make sure she didn't leave anything behind. She spied a hairpin on the sofa and picked it up, putting it in her pocket, all the while avoiding his clear gaze. "I understand, really I do," she went on, realizing belatedly that she was echoing his earlier words. "There's no need to let me down easy with breakfast and such…genteel consideration."

He stood, his lips thinning with disapproval. "Nothing I've done this morning was out of obligation, Mariella."

"Sure it was. You could hardly wake me up and kick me out now could you? That's not very good manners, not when we're supposed to be…what is it we're supposed to be again, Luca?"

She finally looked at him, but his expression was too guarded for her to know what he was thinking.

"I will confess. I'm not sure what is appropriate to say in this situation. It's not one I've been in before."

Luca stared at her. That much was completely true. He'd never been in a situation where he cared more about a woman's feelings than his own. So why was she angry? He'd tried to do the right thing. Look after her, make her day easier, he'd even ordered breakfast for the two of them. He'd wanted to show her that what had transpired yesterday made no difference to him. If anything, it made him respect her more. Everything he'd done…including being here, instead of his office, where he normally would be found at this hour, had been to show her that he cared, that he wasn't running away. He'd wanted to start the day on an even footing.

Now she was furious with him.

Mari started to walk away, her heart sinking. This probably was a new situation for him. He probably kept his affairs nice and neat and clean. She'd needed him so much that she'd obviously imagined things that weren't real. If they had been real, this morning he would have awakened her with a smile. He would have inquired how she was feeling after yesterday and he would have told her it was all right.

And maybe he would have kissed her like she had been aching for him to.

But she'd frightened him off. And he didn't even have the decency to be honest about it.

"I'm leaving now. Thank you for the clothes, but no thank you."

"Where are you going?" Finally there was something in his tone other than perfunctory manners. Mari nearly paused, but made her feet keep going until she reached the door and opened it.

"Mari, we have a meeting with the spa people in an hour."

Mari lifted her chin. "I'm sure you can handle it, Luca. I'm taking the day off."

She went out into the hall and closed the door behind her, without allowing herself to see the expression on his face. She let out a breath she hadn't even known she was holding.

It was time Mari got back to doing what she did best—relying on herself.

CHAPTER TEN

Luca resisted the urge to call her house for the sixth—or was it seventh—time.

He'd been here too long. And nothing had made it more clear than the call he'd had to make earlier this morning, while Mari still slept.

He hadn't known anybody could sleep that long. He kept expecting her to wake throughout the evening, but she hadn't. He'd scrounged through the snacks he kept in his bar and had thrown together what could hardly be considered a meal—bagel chips and some mix made from organic dried fruits.

And at last, around midnight, he'd lain on the sofa, listening for her, finally drifting into a vague sleep.

It was the first time a woman had ever slept in his bed and he hadn't been with her.

At a faint ringing sound, he looked down at his computer screen. Another e-mail from his father, an update on their interest in Paris, which had suffered fire damage. His father had not been pleased at being put off yesterday. And was pressing Luca to finish up and take care of their problems in France.

But it was the words at the end that had him running his fingers through his hair.

Gina's in a mess and Paris can't wait. You need to come back. The family needs you.

The words left an odd ache in him. The family was everything to him. Except…except, he acknowledged, that he'd given his whole life to the family ever since he'd been a boy. He'd been the big brother Gina needed. He'd looked after the household for his father. And he'd wanted to do it. He'd been *happy* to do it. But there were times when he longed to just be Luca. To have his own life, separate from the family. To stop being defined by the Fiori brand. He was growing tired of being at his father's beck and call. Being summoned irritated him.

He typed back: *I will speak to Gina and the manager in Paris. I will come as soon as I can. But my priority is here.*

He signed off and hit Send, then sat back in his chair, rubbing a hand over his mouth. *Dio,* there was more truth in that last line than he'd truly meant. It wasn't just the Cascade that was his priority, though he did consider it his "baby." But it was Mari. She was important.

But what did he want? He'd wanted his own place at Fiori for a very long time. But did what he want match with what Mari wanted? Hardly. Mari wanted

the fairy tale, and he didn't believe in them. The best
thing he could do for her was make sure she kept her
feet on the ground and leave the running of the
Cascade in her capable hands. It wouldn't be enough
for him, but it would be enough for her. Ambition
wasn't Mari's goal, he got that now. She was after
something more substantial. She'd built a life; she
wanted stability, not adventure. It was odd how the
idea appealed to him, especially today. Normally
he'd be thrilled to go to Paris; it was one of his
favorite cities. Now it felt like an imposition,
because he was being *ordered* to go.

And even though he'd sent his response, he knew
he had to leave. Someone from the company had to
put in an appearance. He wasn't clear on what was
wrong with Gina, but he knew his father would be
putting her first. So it was up to Luca to take care
of business.

Yet…how could he possibly say goodbye to Mari
now?

"The Panorama Room is completed. Have you
seen it?"

Mari stopped by his desk. Something was dis-
tracting Luca and she didn't know what it was. She
fiddled with a pen on the top of his blotter. "No, I
haven't made it there today."

Ever since their night together, she'd made sure
she kept her distance. It was clear that Luca cared

for her. He wouldn't have acted so kindly, so gently, if he hadn't cared a little. But she also knew her past was a lot to take on, and their situation wasn't conducive to deep feelings and commitments.

He looked up and smiled, but somehow his heart didn't seem to be in it. "Haven't seen it? You gave me such a difficult time over the decor, and you haven't checked it out yet?" He cleared his throat, rose and shrugged into his jacket. "It can rival any of our dining rooms in any of our facilities, I promise. I've booked the two of us a table for tonight. As a farewell."

"A farewell?"

She paused, unmoving. So soon. She hadn't expected it to be so soon. Her heart sank.

"I've been called to Paris. I leave in the morning."

Luca saw the blood rush from her face and cursed himself. He'd left it an extra day, but he couldn't put it off any longer. Yet the fragile pallor of her skin reminded him of how she'd looked: small and defenseless in his king-size bed. He couldn't shake the image of her sleeping face, the way her hair slid over her pale cheek, the color matching her long eyelashes completely. Couldn't erase the fantasy of that dark sheet of hair falling over his chest as they made love…

He turned away from her abruptly, running a hand over his hair.

"Luca, are you all right?"

He was tired of playing a charade.

This was insane. He wasn't supposed to fall for Mari. A flirtation was one thing, but he didn't intend on having serious feelings for any woman, especially a woman he worked with. And it was clear that Mariella was the *wrong* woman. She was fragile and afraid and trying to overcome something greater than he could comprehend. She deserved a man who could provide her with the stability she needed. Not a man like Luca who flitted from one place to the next.

It would never work between them. And looking at her now…he realized now how it must have seemed to her yesterday. He'd been thinking of himself and putting up walls. He'd been wrong and she'd been right. He'd treated her with no consideration at all. Like he would have a mistress. With politeness, but not genuine caring. He wanted to make it up to her. To show her she was different…because she was.

"I'm fine. I just thought…it's been an eventful few weeks. I thought we could say goodbye with a sense of occasion."

He met her gaze, though it was difficult. She was watching him with eyes wide with compassion and understanding. She only thought she understood. He knew that now.

He would ensure that nothing about his leaving caused Mari further pain. She didn't deserve that, not after all she'd been through. He'd be on his best behavior if it killed him.

He only knew that he had to talk to Mari tonight about how to end their relationship with the least hurt to anyone. He wouldn't be here to protect her, to watch over her if her stepfather decided to find her. The thought chilled his blood and his footsteps faltered. Perhaps he couldn't offer her the life she wanted, but he could damn well make sure she was looked after here.

"That would be lovely, Luca." Her voice was soft, but it cut straight to the heart of him.

"I have some calls to make, first," he said bluntly, and without another word, she left his office, shutting the door behind her.

He picked up the phone and began to put his plans in motion.

Mari studied her reflection with a frown, wondering for the umpteenth time if she should have worn the dress. But the Panorama Room was formal, and she knew the perfect dress was the one she'd bought after their gallery trip. Still heady from Luca's kisses, she'd stared at the dress in the window for only a few seconds before darting inside to try it on. Mari had been under a spell that day, she was sure of it now. The rich scarlet silk of the dress seemed so unlike her, the cut even more daring as it swept from one shoulder down to her waist, leaving the other shoulder bare, the skirt then falling negligently to the floor.

It might have been modest except for the deep slit at the side, revealing her other moment of insanity—the red, sequined slingbacks.

She didn't want to be here. She wasn't sure how to gracefully say goodbye, not when she wanted more. Even when wanting more frightened her so badly her knees were shaking.

Mari swiped a finger beneath her eyelids, wiping away any stray smudges of liner and forcing a smile to the other occupant of the public bathroom.

Her life had been devoid of affection for so long, and she wanted desperately to be romanced. Even if it was only for tonight.

She gathered her pashmina firmly around her and squared her shoulders. It was impossible, she knew that. And caring for Luca as she did and still knowing he wasn't for her gave even a simple farewell dinner a bittersweet taste.

She turned toward the marble stairs and her gaze fell on Luca, waiting for her at the top.

Her heart gave a single, satisfying thump, as if to say, "This is it."

For a few seconds her feet refused to move as their gazes locked. It was something out of a bygone movie as she climbed each of the four stairs, her hand resting on the curve of the elaborate iron railing. The night of shared secrets ceased to exist; the tense atmosphere at breakfast and in the moments since drifted from her memory as she

walked to him, her shoes making tiny clicks on the
Italian veined marble, her breath catching at how
very splendid he looked in evening wear.

At the top he took her hands and kissed each of
her cheeks and her eyes slid closed before she could
think twice. Pulling back slightly, he held out his
arm, and she hesitantly looped hers through his
elbow, awareness and something darker skittering
along her nerve endings as he placed his hand over
her forearm.

"You look…*bellisima*. Beautiful, Mariella. More
beautiful than I can possibly describe."

This was the Luca she remembered, not the practiced stranger from their breakfast, or the distant
boss from this afternoon. Whatever had caused the
change, it was gone and in its place was a man who
exuded warmth and spoke to her as if she were the
only woman in the world. She tried to push the hope
down in her heart, yet a little of it remained. Her
throat tightened as he led her to the door of the
dining room. This was what he'd brought her to,
then. He'd made her *hope* where before there had
been nothing.

Then the door opened and her lips dropped open.

It was more than she'd dreamed, even though
she'd seen the plans. Everything was gilded and
regal, like stepping into a fairy tale with her prince
on her arm. Chandeliers dripped with crystal and
gold; pristine linens a backdrop for the cream and

gold china and the distinctive tinkle of real crystal stemware. Candles flickered in clear, thick pots, covering everything with a luminous, peachy glow. Tuxedoed waitstaff darted between tables amid the hush of opulence.

It was the royal castle Luca had envisioned from the beginning and it was perfect. She knew the end was growing near, yet that little seed of hope in her heart told her it felt like a beginning. "Oh, Luca. Look at what you've done." Her feet stopped moving as she blinked rapidly.

"Not just me. You, Mariella. You inspired this the day you took me to the attic."

"Me?" She turned to him in surprise, found his eyes on her steady and completely in earnest.

"You inspire me, Mariella. Is that so hard to believe?"

"Yes," she whispered, her stomach lifting uncontrollably as his gaze dropped to her mouth. He wouldn't dare kiss her here, would he?

And the moment held, suspended.

He'd been waiting. For *her*. Tonight she wanted to live the fairy tale. To grasp the few fleeting hours and pretend she was the princess. To believe she was chosen. She knew it would end soon enough. Tonight it was hers and she would not ruin it with doubts and fears.

Mari leaned forward slightly, her lips parting, close enough to feel Luca's breath mingle with hers...

"Mr. Fiori? Your table is waiting."

Mari stepped back, her cheeks heating. Luca's arm tightened around her waist and the contact sizzled to her toes.

"Thank you."

Mariella turned around, holding her breath. She was sure now that the gossip mill was probably running overtime ever since she'd been in Luca's suite at nine in the morning. But the hostess's lips dropped open and her eyes lit. "Oh, Ms. Ross! Look at you! You look like a movie star." Realizing her impertinence, she sighed. "Oh, I'm sorry."

Mariella smiled, feeling it light from her toes. "Don't be sorry," Luca answered. "I agree with you. Shall we?"

The hostess led the way into the private dining alcove, the red velvet drapes held back by gold cord. Their table waited, champagne already chilled and ready to pour. As she sat, she beamed up at him. "Luca, this is amazing. I've never seen anything quite like it, you know. I certainly never expected it here. In what was the Bow Valley Inn."

He poured the champagne, handing each of them a glass. "To remarkable transformations," he murmured, touching his rim to hers.

Glasses clinked and Mari drank the dry, fizzy champagne, feeling more with every moment that she was in a dream…a good one this time…and that at any moment she'd awake and the spell would be broken.

First courses arrived, then second; more champagne was drunk and Mari made sure she put her glass down more frequently as things grew fuzzy and warm around the edges. Luca laughed as he recounted stories of his youth with Gina; escapades with each other and Luca's winery friend Dante who to all accounts sounded like a rebel and usually in the middle of any trouble. She alternated between feeling a beautiful sense of belonging at being privy to the memories, and an acute sadness of the sort of childhood she'd missed. She didn't have any of the sorts of memories they did, of close times and scrapes and fun. Then Luca laughed and touched her hand beneath the table and she shook off any lingering sadness. She'd learned to live in the moment a long time ago. This was no time to start having regrets or wishing for what had never been.

They were served dark chocolate terrine drizzled with raspberry coulis when Luca leaned forward and captured Mari's hand.

Mari sat up straighter, startled at the sudden, personal gesture. But Luca was completely sincere as he squeezed Mari's fingers.

"When I arrived, I only wanted to do one thing— transform the hotel into something more Fiori. But my time here has been so much more, Mari, and I have you to thank for that."

Mari couldn't reply. Her gaze darted to Luca's; his gaze was sincere. It was no protestation of love, but only a fool would expect such a thing. His statement was absolutely correct. It had been more than either of them expected. She would have to be happy with that. Luca was not in love with her. And she'd get over him in time. She would.

But she returned the handclasp with as much warmth as she had inside her. "It has been a pleasure getting to know you, Luca. And getting to know myself better. I owe you so much. I'm only sorry I don't know how to repay you."

She had fought him tooth and nail in the beginning. And then somehow he'd gotten under her skin and she'd let him see a side of her she'd never revealed to anyone before. And in trusting him, she'd fallen in love with him.

Dessert was over, and the last bit had felt like a goodbye. Mari moved to collect her handbag, but Luca put out a hand. "Where are you going?"

She looked up, confused. "Home? I thought dinner was over."

Luca tugged on her arm gently, pulling her closer. "I'm not ready for it to end yet."

With his free hand he reached out and flicked the ties on the drapes, closing them in a cocoon of velvet and candlelight.

"Luca—"

"I need to say something here," he interrupted whatever it was she was going to say. "I'm sorry about yesterday morning, Mariella. I was unbearable and I have no excuse. I can only say that I meant well and realize now how it must have seemed to you."

She would not cry. She wouldn't spoil this beautiful evening with tears, no matter how angry or hurt she'd been only hours before. The moment he had kissed her cheeks tonight she'd known that yesterday morning hadn't been real. He'd been putting on a show. A very effective one. His apology meant more than he knew.

Their bodies hovered closer together, but Mari resisted the urge to take the one step necessary to be pressed against him. "It was a lot to take in at once, Luca. I was hurt by your behavior, but only because I understood. My story isn't the stuff of polite chitchat. Your reaction made sense."

"But you don't understand, Mari, that's the thing. You don't understand anything."

It was Luca who took the step and Mari found her breasts pressed against the fabric of his suit coat. Without thinking she lifted her hand, the silky fabric of her pashmina drifting off her shoulder and hanging from her right elbow. Her finger traced the hard angle of his jaw. "Then help me understand."

He didn't answer. Instead he reached up and gripped her wrist with his hand and lowered his mouth to hers.

She opened her lips, letting his tongue sweep inside, tasting the tangy sharpness of fine champagne and the dark seduction of cool chocolate.

With his other hand he dragged her closer. The clinking sounds of the dining room echoed behind them, slightly muffled by the seclusion of the alcove. Luca's lips trailed over her cheek to her ear and down the curve of her neck, dropping feather-light kisses that made her weak in the knees and destroyed any resolve she might have had.

"Luca," she uttered, shattered, wondering what it would be like to give herself to a man for the first time since that awful day seven years before. To feel safe and protected. Cherished.

"The first time I saw you, your hair was up." He whispered against her temple and sank her fingers into her waves. "And I knew that moment that one day you'd wear it down and you'd look exactly like you do tonight. *Bellissima* Mariella."

She tilted her head back, feeling her hair slide along her shoulder blades as his mouth followed the curve of her neckline toward her collarbone. There was no reason for him to be touching her this way unless…unless…

Sensation after sensation swirled through her: touch, taste, the feel of his body holding hers and the taste of his lips as their mouths clashed again. His fingers found the zipper at the back of her dress and lowered it a few inches, sliding his fingers along the seam while Mari ached to be touched. It ceased to matter where they were.

But he stepped back.

"I can't do this Mari. It's not fair."

Her body still vibrated from his embrace. "I don't understand."

Gently he reached out, picked up the trailing end of her shawl and placed it over her naked shoulder. "I cannot be with you tonight knowing that tomorrow…"

He hesitated, the silence so terrible Mari thought she would certainly scream. Finally she broke the silence with the one question she had wanted to ask since this morning but hadn't had the courage to hear the answer.

"When will you be back?"

For the first time that evening, his gaze skittered away. "I have no plans to return. Once Paris is looked after, I am returning to Florence for the holiday with my family."

A family that didn't include her. No matter how welcome she'd felt in his arms, it came down to the resounding fact that she was an outsider.

And with that, everything went sinking to her toes.

It was clear. Despite what they'd shared, despite the attraction that clearly simmered between them—she knew that much to be true—there wasn't enough to keep him here. She stood motionless, not sure of what to say. Until she'd asked the question, there had been a tiny flicker of hope. But she'd only been fooling herself. She had *always* known he was leaving, so why was she feeling so betrayed? Why was she feeling like somehow she'd failed?

Because she wasn't ready to let him go yet. That was what he'd done to her. He'd shown her herself and he'd taught her to hope. And in the process he'd ended up breaking her heart by doing what he'd said he was going to all along. Leaving.

She should have known better. Should have thought it through more. Should have realized that in the end they couldn't just go their separate ways like nothing had happened.

"Say something, Mari."

She sat down in the chair. "There is nothing to say, Luca. We both knew this time was coming. I guess I just hoped you'd be back."

"We knew this was temporary."

She couldn't tell him how she'd grown to care for him, to rely on him. It would sound weak and clingy and that wasn't what she wanted. It was irrelevant now anyway. Tomorrow he'd be gone. There was no sense fighting what was obviously not meant to be.

"I thought you'd be around to supervise more of the refurbishing, that's all."

His jaw relaxed a little and he sat, too, turning his chair to face her. "I did, too. The plan was for me to be here several more weeks. But I'm needed more elsewhere...I know I'm leaving the Cascade in capable hands, Mari. And I'm only a phone call or e-mail away if you need help. I have full confidence in you."

The words were hollow. He was leaving the rest of the job to her. He believed in her ability to run his hotel. She supposed she should be happy about that, but instead it simply felt wrong, doing it without him.

"I also spoke to my father today and we're making you the permanent manager of the Fiori Cascade."

It was what she'd wanted, what she'd aimed for since moving to Banff and taking the administration job. Now it felt like the consolation prize. When had she started wanting more?

She looked down at her knees. She knew when. When she'd stopped giving Robert all the power and she'd started living for herself.

"Thank you, Luca. It's…it's what I wanted and I appreciate your faith in me. I won't let you down."

Luca stared at her dark head and wondered how the hell he'd screwed this up so spectacularly.

He should have kept things as he had this morning. Cool and businesslike.

Mari was important to him. Somehow he'd let her become important and that wasn't fair to either of them. And he'd tried to remind himself of that all day. Instead he'd lost his head when he'd seen her come up those stairs looking so elegant in her gown. She moved with an easy, subtle grace that spoke of a little shyness. But Mari was not coy. She did not play games. And he'd wanted her on his arm as he'd never wanted any other woman to belong to him. Not even Ellie.

And he'd kissed her and touched her and ached to make love to her so badly he'd nearly lost himself. Until he realized he didn't have the right to hurt her. And he knew her well enough now to know that to love her once and leave her behind would be the most selfish thing he could do.

The best thing he could do for her would be to give her what she'd wanted from the beginning…the running of the hotel. It didn't matter that he wasn't completely happy himself. His father's summons had irritated him from the first moment. He was tired of being at the beck and call of his father and knew now he wanted more. Yet…his first loyalty was to his family and to the Fiori empire. He'd made his choice years ago. He couldn't have both.

"You could never let me down, Mari, never." No, he was the one letting her down and it hurt like hell.

He fingered the ring on his hand, the gold one with the lily emblazoned upon it.

"That ring is important to you, isn't it." Her voice was quiet now, the soft tones burning through him like a brand. "I've never seen you without it on."

He nodded, resting his hands on his knees. Perhaps if he explained about the ring she'd understand why he had to go. "My grandmother gave it to my grandfather. It went on to become the Fiori crest—beauty, loyalty, strength."

"You have such a history, Luca, I envy that."

"Sometimes it's not all that it seems," he replied quickly, then shook his head. His issues with Fiori weren't Mari's to solve. "I just mean that with it comes responsibility. I have a duty to my family, and it's the life I was given, as well as the life I chose. It anchors me."

"But…"

He had to be very careful. He'd give anything not to hurt her yet he knew he must. He should have known better.

He got up and walked to the end of the table, stopping and closing his eyes for a moment.

When he turned back he held out his hand and she took it. He marveled again at how soft and small hers was compared to his.

"We both knew I wasn't here forever, and we both knew my job would take me away." He inhaled, bracing himself for a small truth he could spare. "We also know that what we shared is special. You are special, Mari."

"You'll forget all about me." She turned her head away. "I'll just be another one of those women you once knew."

"Don't do that. It cheapens what we've shared."

She peered back into his face. "You actually sound like you mean that."

"I do." He lifted her fingers and kissed them. "I care about you so much. And yet…the time has come as we knew it would, and I must go back to my life and you are here in yours. There really is no other choice. I simply want us to part without bitterness, but with a respect for what was between us. For you to know that it…"

He paused. He could get through this. Even if explaining it was one of the hardest things he'd ever done.

He met her gaze with his and made the decision to be as honest as he could. "To know that it meant something to me."

"You are making it very difficult to be angry with you," she choked, half a laugh and half a sob.

"If it is easier for you to be angry with me, then so be it. I only want your happiness, Mari."

And for the first time in his life, he knew it was true. He wanted her happiness ahead of his own. And a flash of fear: never did he want to become his father. Papa had dedicated his life to his wife's happiness only to have it mean nothing. Luca had seen how Papa had been destroyed when his mother left them all. He also remembered the exact moment when his own innocence, his own belief in happy endings was so cruelly broken. And he knew now that it was nothing compared to the power Mari could have over his heart.

She turned away and wiped a finger beneath her lashes, catching the tear before it could trickle down her cheek. How could she explain that somehow her happiness was now bound up in him, too? He was right about everything! How they had both known this time would come. But she remembered being held in his arms as she'd explained about Robert and feeling safe and loved. All that would go with him when he went away. She'd utterly despised him that first day in her office, and now she'd give anything to have him stay.

"And I want yours," she replied. She looked up into his eyes, wishing she were in his arms once more. It suddenly struck her that she wouldn't kiss him ever again and a surge of emptiness engulfed her. All this time she'd fought to go back to her old life. And faced with it now, it seemed cold and pointless.

"Luca?"

His fingers were gripping hers so tightly they pained.

"Will you kiss me one more time?"

She heard the plea in her voice but for once didn't care. She stood and walked into his embrace, felt his hands gently cup her neck as his lips grazed her temple.

She barely breathed, her chest rising and falling in shallow breaths as his mouth toyed with hers, treating her like precious china. Her lids drifted closed as the soft skin of his lips touched the crest of her cheek, her forehead, her lashes before tentatively settling on her mouth. The kiss there shattered her with its innocence and purity. Her wrap floated to the floor but she didn't care. Three little words hovered on her lips but she held them in. There was something tenuous and fragile between them and Mari would not break that connection by voicing protestations of love. Instead she kept the words treasured in her heart until it hurt so much she knew she had to leave before breaking down completely.

"I need to go," she gasped, pulling back and grappling for her purse. "I'm sorry. I can't do this."

She rushed out of the alcove before Luca could utter a single word.

Luca bent and picked up the wrap she'd left behind, turning it over in his fingers. Mariella, with her innocent pleas and courageous heart.

Summons be damned. He'd come here tonight to reinstate the status quo with Mari and all he'd done was stir things up more. He ran a hand over his face. He'd never had this trouble before. He was good at moving on. And he couldn't figure out why this time was different.

He'd simply let himself get too involved, that was all. He was just being a fool, thinking this was love. He folded the wrap and gripped the soft fabric in his hand. Maybe she wouldn't see it now, but his leaving was the best thing for both of them.

CHAPTER ELEVEN

THE house was dark when Mari entered. Times like this her heart always beat a little faster; no matter how much she told herself the past was over, she knew it really wasn't. She'd always have that little bit of fear lurking behind dark and closed doors. It was simple preoccupation that had caused her to forget to leave a few lights burning. As soon as she stepped inside, she flicked on the kitchen light, the instant glow alleviating some of her anxiety.

Luca was leaving. All the turmoil of the past weeks would be gone, like they'd never happened. She was getting her life back. It was what she wanted.

Aimlessly she let her fingers drift over the mail she'd brought in earlier and had thrown on the table in her distraction of getting ready for dinner. Her fingers paused over an odd white-and-red envelope that meant Express service…and opened it to find another letter-size envelope bearing an insignia and the words Toronto Police Service.

She held the letter in trembling hands. After a few

minutes of staring at it, she turned it over, ripped the flap and pulled out a single sheet of paper.

It was over.

Mariella sat heavily in the kitchen chair, the paper still open and shaking in her fingers. Tommy's nails tapped on the floor and he sat beside her, putting his head down on her knee. The warmth from it soaked into her leg, anchoring her to the present.

This was her life. Hers. And now, *hers alone*. The past was gone, melted away in a few short paragraphs.

She had to read it once more to make sure it was true.

Dear Ms Ross,

I am writing to inform you of the death of Robert Langston.

He died on November 25, when the vehicle he was driving left the road and overturned. Alcohol was determined a factor in the crash.

Mari wiped away tears. He was gone. He had no power to hurt her anymore.

She kept reading, the rest scrawled in semi-neat handwriting at the bottom of the page.

I know this isn't procedure, but I wanted to notify you myself. As the arresting officer in the original case, I have often thought of you and your mother. Some cases are like that. I can

only say that I hope you are well and that perhaps this might provide some sort of resolution
for you and Mrs. Langston.
    Sincerely,
    Cst. Pat Moore

She remembered Constable Moore. He'd been
steady, firm, gentle when questioning her at the
hospital and then later when he'd testified at
the trial. Somehow, having him be the one to break
the news brought things full circle, even through
something as simple as a letter. She wondered
briefly if her mother was somewhere tonight,
reading an identical letter, feeling the same
relief…and regret.

Her first instinct was to tell Luca.

Mari looked up, swiping a finger under her lashes.
Telling Luca was the last thing she should do,
though. They'd all but said goodbye tonight. And
he'd dealt with her problems enough. No, it was
time to stand on her own two feet. The fact that she
could…and be worry free…was a heady thought.

Standing, she walked over to where the painting
he'd given her hung. She skimmed her fingers over
the surface, the letter dangling from her opposite
hand. She knew now what she hadn't been able to
put together the day she'd first seen it. She knew now
not only that it had spoken to her, but what it said.

It was life; the life in her that he'd awakened.

The life she'd fought for every step of the way. And it bled on the canvas and she realized that by living, by feeling, she'd also opened herself up to hurt. And the shocking, glorious realization that it had been worth it.

Tears trickled down her cheeks. She had sworn up and down that she'd moved on from the wounds Robert had inflicted on her, but that wasn't true. She'd only covered them up. And then she'd met Luca and he'd made her face them, and he'd made her fall in love with him.

Only she'd been so crippled she hadn't had the courage to fight for him. Even tonight she'd simply accepted what he'd said—that he was leaving.

She took the letter, crumpled it into a ball and threw it into the fire.

Over the past weeks she'd wondered if she'd only been attracted to Luca because of Robert and what he'd done to her. She'd asked herself if she'd felt such an attachment because he seemed to protect her from her fear. Wondered if she'd been receptive to him because she'd needed him to make her feel safe after Robert had been released.

But it wasn't true, none of it.

As the paper curled and flamed, reducing to ash, she knew without a doubt that she was free. And that freedom did absolutely nothing to release her from the longing she had for Luca.

The painting brought it all back, fresh and new. Luca's smile, his eyes, the way he challenged her and pushed her and kissed her. The way he'd gotten her to talk about her abuse and how she'd come to rely on him.

But the man who had made her life a living hell, who had beaten her mother and then her, who had put her in the hospital for weeks and who had caused years of therapy…was suddenly gone.

She no longer had to look around corners. She no longer had to deal with updates from parole officers, victim impact statements, or worry if he'd try to find her or if he'd come back to finish the job. She'd had no doubt that he was capable of it. And there was a little bit of guilt in the fact that a man had to die for her to feel free of her own personal prison.

She was rid of Robert Langston and she had the job, the life, she'd always wanted.

And somehow, she still felt completely empty.

She straightened her shoulders. As if preordained, the words of the note that had accompanied the painting rang in her ears: "When it speaks to your heart, you know it's the right one."

She'd been so very utterly wrong.

It hadn't been about Robert. It was about Luca. He was the one that spoke to her heart. He was the right one. She could either accept what he'd said tonight or she could fight for him. And she had no idea if she was brave enough to go through with it.

* * *

There had been no chance to speak privately. With Luca planning on leaving so soon, the morning was completely filled with meetings and details. Mari looked across the table at him. The sinking feeling that had begun last night widened to a gulf that threatened to swallow her up.

It wasn't about drapes and fixtures and figures anymore.

She already felt the loss of him and didn't know how she was going to manage it when he was gone. And she had no confidence at all in her ability to convince him to stay.

Something had changed. The sound of his voice as he hashed things over with the plumbing contractor both grounded her and filled her with emptiness. Never, in the seven years since she'd been attacked, had she let down her guard so completely. She'd been so used to reacting to things that she didn't know how to take control and act. And while he thought that giving her control of the Cascade was what she wanted, nothing was further from the truth. A month ago she would have taken it gladly. But now…it meant nothing, not without Luca.

But it wasn't what they agreed, and she had spent the better part of the morning desperately trying to find a time to speak to him in private to tell him that she'd changed.

Luca wound up the meeting and shook hands with the contractor. Mari smiled and offered her hand as well, knowing that from this moment on she would be the one carrying out Luca's vision. She was pleased he trusted her enough to leave her with it. No one had ever shown her that much faith before. But at what cost? She wanted them to do it together. They had thus far and it had changed her life. The last thing she wanted was to go back to her old life. It was drab and colorless now.

The door to the conference room had just closed and Mari turned, wanting to say something and not knowing what. For a few long seconds their eyes clashed and she wished she knew how to put into words what she was feeling.

Mari straightened her blouse. Should she ask him to lunch? Suggest something else? Her stomach twisted.

"That covers it, then." His voice came quietly across the room and she closed her eyes, wondering if she could take the sound of it and commit it to memory.

"Piece of cake," she replied, trying to inject some vigor into her words. They fell flat.

"Mari, I…"

"Luca, would…"

They both halted as they interrupted each other. He held out his hand, offering to let her go first.

Always the gentleman.

"I was wondering if you'd like to have some lunch before you leave for the airport."

"Do you think that's wise?"

Mari shook her head. Would she feel better or worse for it? "Probably not. But I'm tired of being wise."

The air crackled between them. She didn't look away, couldn't. She wanted to remember how he looked in his Italian suits, remember the sound of his voice, the way his cologne smelled. Wanted to imprint everything about him on her memory. She'd thought they had time, but after last night, the sand in the hourglass was slipping away much too quickly.

From the moment he'd stepped up and defended her, something had snapped, had turned around. Perhaps it was ridiculous, but she'd felt part of a unit. That with him beside her Robert couldn't hurt her anymore. She loved him for that. Loved him for giving her safety, and freedom. He was her asylum.

Now he was taking it away, and she refused to accept it. She didn't need asylum anymore. Robert was gone. He had no power over her now. And she wanted Luca more than ever before.

"Mari." He leaned back against the conference table and folded his arms. His lips were unsmiling, troubled. "Mari, if we do this it won't change anything. I'm still leaving."

"Don't."

"Don't what?" He looked confused and his arms unfolded. "Don't say goodbye? Would you rather I left without a word?"

Mari swallowed every single ounce of fear and lifted her eyes to his. "Don't go."

He sighed. "You'll be fine here. You don't need me."

She shook her head. She'd opened the door and damn it, she was going to walk through it.

"I do need you. More than you know. Robert…"

Luca's back came away from the wall. "Robert what? Did he contact you?" His hands gripped her elbows and she tried to ignore the thrill that shot through her, just having him this close. "Is he trying to find you? I swear, Mari, if he…"

Mari shook her head quickly. "No, no! Of course not… Luca, Robert is *dead*."

Luca released her arms and stared at her dumbly. She started to laugh at his confounded expression.

"I'm sorry. But you should see your face."

"How did it happen?"

"Car accident. I opened the letter when I got home last night."

Luca came forward and hugged her, surprising her with the strength of the embrace. "I'm glad. Oh that sounds awful, doesn't it? But I was worried about you. I told Vince…"

Mari pulled away. "You told Vince what?" Vince was their head of security, and she'd hired him herself two years earlier.

"I told him to keep an eye on you. To make sure you were protected."

"And why does that matter to you?"

"How can you ask that?" He nearly exploded, spinning around and going behind the table, putting it between them.

Mari smiled and leaned slightly over the polished top. "I *am* asking that very thing. Why does my protection matter to you?"

"Because I…" He faltered and then scowled. "You know why."

Oh, her Luca. He'd helped her more in a few short weeks than months of therapy ever had. She didn't know how she could ever explain how much that meant. She knew in her heart she couldn't let him go without a fight, so for the first time in her life, she stopped hiding in the shadows and came out to face her fear head-on.

She let all her love for him shine out of her eyes. "Yes, I think I know why." She straightened, folded her hands demurely and said with far more confidence than she felt: "Then stay. I love you, Luca. Stay with me and love me back."

Nothing she could have said could have affected him more. His heart pounded at her words for a brief moment of elation before reality kicked in.

And in some small corner of his mind, he heard voices from his past. Voices asking for love and having it denied. Of going through the motions until it just wasn't enough. He wasn't fool enough to believe Mari actually meant it. And even if he did love her back—which he couldn't possibly—it would be impossible for him to say the words.

"Mari, I don't know what to say." He knew he sounded cold and wished it were different. "I know what we said last night, about it meaning something, that was all true. But love…" His voice trailed away. He couldn't say the words that leaped into his brain. *I'm not ready for love.*

"You've been through a horrible ordeal, and I think if you take time to look at it rationally, you'll see your feelings are misplaced gratitude."

"I do owe you thanks," she agreed, and from the way she worried her fingers he could tell this wasn't coming easily for her. "For showing me how to feel again, Luca. For forcing me out of my box and into the world again."

Oh, what had he done! His brilliant plans. Never had he considered they would end like this!

"I don't need your gratitude."

She drew back and he tried hard to ignore the hurt his jab had caused. It was written all over her face.

"You're turning me away."

He came around the table and took her icy hand in his. He'd give anything not to be breaking her heart right now, but he couldn't give her what she wanted. He didn't know how. He'd fought against it his whole life! He couldn't just change who he was in an instant, just because she asked him to.

He remembered how she'd cried on his chest and poured out her pain. Hated himself for how much he wanted to stay and hold her that way. She'd made him weak. That's what she'd done to him without even trying. And because he knew she hadn't meant to do it, he placed all the blame firmly on himself for becoming vulnerable to her. And for giving her hope where he shouldn't have.

He squeezed her fingers. "I meant what I said last night. We did have a connection, you and me. We just knew it wasn't forever. I will always look back on this as a fond memory."

He didn't know how to handle her tears, but to his surprise she pulled her hands away from his and straightened her shoulders.

"A fond memory. That's all." She tried a smile but he saw through it to how deeply he'd hurt her and regret had a bitter taste.

He had to get out now before he made a huge fool of himself or hurt her feelings further. There really was no choice. He was due in Paris. He'd given his word he'd be there and he'd never broken a promise to his father, even when he'd wanted to. Yet he couldn't quite bring himself to break ties with the Cascade, either. Changing it, restoring it, had meant a great deal to him and he hated having to walk away from all their hard work. It was more than a project. It was his and Mari's project. At least he knew that he was leaving it in good hands.

"I'm sorry you thought it was more. I'll be in touch anyway, about the hotel. So this isn't really goodbye."

"That's all you have to say?" Her blue eyes blazed up at him, looking for truth and he didn't have any to give.

"Yes, that's all."

"This is goodbye, then. After everything."

He nodded. Perhaps it was kinder to let her go angry. Maybe it would make it easier for her to move on. His stomach burned acidly at the thought, but he carried on. "Yes. I assured my father I'd be in Paris as soon as I could. I'm leaving with Charlie within the hour."

She held out her hand. "Goodbye, Luca. It's been a pleasure working with you."

He took her hand and felt the trembling there.

"Goodbye, Mariella."

She pulled her hand away and retrieved her purse. She walked down the hall and out the doors, through the parking garage to her car.

And once she was inside, she finally let it all go in a rash of weeping. She'd risked it all. And lost.

CHAPTER TWELVE

DAWN wasn't gray; it was pure white.

Mari looked out the window and shook her head. Last night she hadn't given a thought to a storm, but at this time of year anything could happen in the mountains. Should she go in to work, or take a day off? It was a short drive, but her road hadn't been cleared and she wasn't sure her little car could handle the curves. Not to mention the return drive, up the hill. Flakes were still falling in thick pads, obscuring the view of even the parking area above the cottage.

Tommy came back in from his trip to the yard, shaking the snow from his golden coat with great enthusiasm. Mari gave him an absent pat and went to the bathroom. Seeing her puffy eyes in the mirror, she decided that there were advantages to being the boss. She made the necessary call—they'd be running on essential staff today anyway—and decided she could work from home this once. She would log in to the server at the hotel and access all her files, and if anything was pressing Becky could phone.

She put on the coffeepot and calculated the time difference in Paris. It was afternoon there already. What was he doing?

Before long, he'd be in Italy, with his father and Gina and her children. All she'd wanted when he'd walked in that first morning was to get rid of him and retain her manager's job. And now she'd done it. And knew that the sad reality was that yesterday she'd been prepared to give it all up if only he would have said he loved her back.

She was starting on her second cup of coffee when a knock sounded at the door. She opened it to find Luca there, bundled in a heavy parka with Bow Valley Inn embroidered on the front. It was obvious he'd raided the old boutique storage for suitable outerwear.

"Luca!"

"Can I come in?"

She had been so shocked to see him that she'd been standing in the doorway like a dolt. "Of course! How did you… when are…I mean, what happened to your flight?"

He stepped inside, his already tall figure made even larger by the addition of winter boots and the jacket. "I didn't take it," he replied, pulling a black toque off his head and shoving it into a pocket. His normally precisely gelled hair was in disarray from the hat. To Mari, he'd never looked better.

And she was suddenly acutely aware that she

stood before him, barefoot and braless in a pair of pink candy-striped flannel pyjamas.

"Oh Lord, excuse me a moment!" Her cheeks went hot as his gaze remained pinned to her flannel jammies.

"Mariella," he said, and her feet refused to move.

Just yesterday he'd said goodbye. He'd taken her protestation of love and had politely, but quite definitively, rejected it. Why was he here now?

"I couldn't get on that plane."

"You couldn't?"

He shook his head. And she frantically tried to beat down the hope that fluttered in her heart. There was no sense getting her hopes up. They'd said all there was to say. He'd been crystal clear.

He unzipped his coat, shrugging out of it. When he stood there with it in his hands, it came to her that she should hang it up for him.

"I'm glad you didn't go into the office today. The roads are horrid."

"Yet you came here." She turned from the closet, amazed at herself for voicing the thought so easily. A month ago she would never have done such a thing. It was more proof just how much she'd changed since Luca had come to the Cascade. She owed him more than he knew, for shaking her out of her life that had been nothing more than self-preservation.

"I have the four-wheel drive. You only have your little car."

"I called in to say I was doing paperwork from home. I should get dressed…"

"Mari wait." The urgency in those two words stopped her.

"I came here to say things. Things I should have said yesterday. But you caught me off guard."

He bent, removed his boots and padded across the hardwood to stand before her.

"My Mariella," he whispered, lifting a hand to her cheek and cupping it.

"Don't," she choked, her eyes drifting shut anyway. "Luca, I can't take it. You said all you needed to yesterday."

But he ignored her, cupped her other cheek and dropped the sweetest of kisses on her eyelids.

"That's where you're wrong. I said too much, and all the wrong things. You, Mariella Ross, made me a coward, and that's not something I like in myself."

His breath was warm on her forehead. "You're not afraid of anything," she whispered breathlessly.

"I'm afraid of you. I'm afraid of me, how I feel when I'm with you. And then on the drive to Calgary I realized how incredibly difficult it must have been for you to say what you did. And how you deserved better from me."

She leaned back, searched his eyes. "And that's why you're here?"

"That's what frightens me, Mari. You make me

want to give you more. You make me want to be worthy and I'm terrified of failing. Again."

"I don't understand."

He tugged on her hand and led her to the table and chairs that covered the space between the kitchen and living room. When she was seated he pulled a chair close and sat so that their knees were pressed together, the same way he had the night she'd told him about Robert.

"Mari, you deserve so much more than what I have to give. I hadn't even given a thought to love, and everything that goes with that. You're just now stepping out of the shadow of all you've been through. I said what I did because I was too selfish to end it like I wanted to. I wanted us to stay friends, and if not that, business associates that had shared something great."

His thumbs grazed her knees. "You make me want things, things I haven't wanted for a very long time. I thought I was making the right decision by leaving. For you, for me. I thought my reasons were right. But I was wrong. I had Charlie bring me back. And I spent all of last night trying to fix it."

"You have to go to Paris."

"No, *cara.* I don't."

He took her hands in his. She wanted to believe him, even when his words of yesterday still rang in her ears. He was here and for some reason being here was important. She had to believe that was because somehow *she* was important.

She absorbed how he looked; the tanned skin, the full mouth that didn't smile, the cappuccino-colored eyes that had always been able to see into her. Somewhere along the way he'd become her ideal. She longed to cup his face in her hands and kiss him as he'd kissed her that last night in the alcove.

But he spoke, keeping her in her chair.

"You know that my mother left my father when I was very young. And though we had our father, I felt very responsible for Gina. And for my father at times as well, because I was old enough to see how our mother leaving had hurt him. Time and again I saw him ask for her love and she gave it, but the words were meaningless. He tried in every way he could but it wasn't enough for her."

"Did you think I didn't mean what I said yesterday?"

"I'm not one for words, Mari. I need to be shown…I need to show. I said the words once…remember I told you about Ellie. I gave her my heart. And it wasn't so much that I found her with someone else, you see. It wasn't even that I learned she was only with me because I was a Fiori. It was that I'd trusted her, with my heart. It was my judgment holding me back. And I vowed not to trust it again. So when I started having feelings for you, I gave myself every justification and excuse in the book."

Mari pictured a younger Luca, vibrant with being in love and having that crushed. She squeezed his fingers. "So you focused on work."

"There was never a question of me working for Fiori. It is my heritage. A heritage built by my grandparents. I would feel I had let them down if I hadn't stayed with the company. I would have felt as if I'd let myself down. I love Fiori. It is in my blood."

"I hear a 'but' in there."

He let out a little sigh. "But I spent many years focusing on my job alone, avoiding people. And I didn't know how to have both."

She raised an eyebrow. She had the magazines to prove that his nonavoidance was well documented. Yet she knew he did have it within him. The way he'd held her as she cried proved it. Luca was capable of great feeling.

"Oh," he chuckled, a smile flirting at the corners of his mouth. "I did put on a good show. But I never got close to anyone after Ellie. Never wanted to. Gina got married and started a family and I kept traveling around the world, watching out for our interests. But putting on a front takes a lot of energy, Mariella. You, of all people know that."

She rested a hand on his arm. "Yes, I do. You always seemed so self-assured, Luca. I never would have guessed you were unhappy."

"And I wasn't, not really. There was simply something missing." He put his hand over hers. "I was missing roots. Which sounds foolish considering how I just told you how my family grounds me."

"There's a big difference between coming from roots and finding your own place." Mari gazed into his eyes. "I know I'll never have the former. I never knew my real father and my childhood was a nightmare. But…but I think I've made a place for myself here."

"I know you have. I know it because I could see it from the beginning. You belong here. You fit. You fit in a way I never seemed to." He looked around the cottage. "I can see you within these walls. You've made this into a home, one that is only yours."

"It doesn't mean I'm not lonely."

"Are you lonely, Mari?"

She bit her lower lip and nodded slightly. "Yes, yes, I am. At least I was, and never knew it. You changed that for me."

"I never expected to find you, you see." He grabbed her hand, lifting it and kissing her fingers. "And when I did, I still didn't believe in it. I didn't trust in it. I had feelings for you but I pushed them away, pretended they weren't real. I told myself it was temporary and that I'd go back to Italy and I would be fine. And then you told me you loved me."

"I do love you."

He looked down then, for several seconds. When he lifted his head, he said simply, "You humble me, Mari."

He leaned forward and rested his forehead against hers.

"You, the one who had every right to be afraid…you're the one who has taught me. You're my miracle, Mariella. And I'm terrified you'll get up one day and realize I'm not good enough for you."

Tears clogged her throat. She couldn't imagine being anyone's miracle. Not after where she came from. After all she'd endured.

"I fell in love with you, and I thought you only needed me because of your stepfather."

She swiped a finger beneath her lashes. "Oh, Luca, how could you think that?"

"I wanted to be the one to make you see, but then you did and I couldn't bear the thought of you with anyone else. And I knew you deserved more than me and nothing made sense. Until you were gone yesterday and it all became very, very, clear."

"It had nothing to do with Robert and everything to do with me," she assured him. "You were the first person to see beyond what he'd done to me. The first person to make me forget and make me feel like it didn't matter. The first person to make me feel like the real Mariella. You could never disappoint me, Luca. *Never.*"

He rested his elbows on his knees, his hands on the outside of her thighs now. She smiled; when he'd arrived he'd had a penchant for touching that she couldn't stand and now she couldn't get enough.

"I've grown weary of all the travel. I have a villa, but I'm rarely there. When I was younger it was exciting. I never wanted to settle down. I thought I had life by the tail. But things change. *I* changed. I started to hate having to drop things at a moment's notice. I enjoyed building the business—being here with you and reimagining the Cascade was wonderful. And then…then my father called the morning after you told me about Robert and said I was being sent to Paris right away."

A wistful smile fluttered on her lips. "That was why you acted the way you did?"

"There was so much going on with me. I was suddenly involved with you on a much deeper level than I was prepared for, and it scared me. I wanted to show you that none of it mattered to me. And then on the other hand was my father telling me I had to leave and I resented the order. I'd put him off the day before and it didn't go over well with him. And I wanted to make a change and didn't know how, and it was all tied in with these feelings for my family and for you."

It all was starting to make sense.

"I was certain that leaving was the best thing. I didn't want to be in love. I didn't want to put myself in the position of letting someone hurt me."

Mari couldn't believe she'd ever had that kind of power. Yet here he was, clasping her hands, telling her how he felt and with every passing moment the crack he'd opened in her heart grew wider.

"I've never been in love before, either," she admitted. "But it came down to knowing I'd regret it for the rest of my life. I had to tell you. And I had to ask you to love me back."

His tongue slid out to wet his lips and Mari's pulse thudded.

"I want to kiss you right now," he murmured huskily, "but I need to tell you the rest first."

"Then hurry."

She breathed the response and again she felt the tug between them, the one she hadn't imagined all those weeks ago.

"I spoke to my father. About Fiori, about my discontent, about you. And we talked about my mother."

"You did?"

"A child's wounds take a long time to heal, don't you think? He forgave her long ago. But I never did. I always carried this bitterness with me. It made me jaded. But I need to move past it. If you can move past Robert, surely I can find a way to forgive my mother."

Tears burned on her lashes. "You're not the only one, Luca. I've been thinking about my own mother a lot lately. How can I judge her for making decisions out of fear, when I did the same thing for years?" Their hands were joined and she ran her thumbs along the base of his. "I'm going to try to find her again. I'm pretty sure the police officer that sent the letter will help me."

They sat quietly for a moment, letting it all digest. All the changes in both of them, each brought on by the love from the other. Finally Luca spoke.

"When all was said and done, by the end of the conversation I'd resigned my position and had taken a new one. As vice president and in charge of Fiori's North American resorts. I'll be managing everything on this side of the Atlantic, from one main office."

"How wonderful for you, Luca. What a fabulous job!" She smiled yet wasn't sure how to react or exactly what it meant. North America was a big continent.

He sighed, pulling away and running a hand through his hair. "*Dio,* you're tough." He regarded her with sharp eyes before finally coming out with it. "Would you be happy anywhere else, Mari? Could you leave this place behind?"

Could she do it for Luca? She looked around her little cottage, the home she'd built from nothing. Could she leave it behind her? If it meant being with him, she knew she could.

"Yes."

"But you wouldn't want to. You do love it here."

"Of course I do, but…I'm not sure what you're asking of me. Or what exactly has happened."

"My priorities changed, that's what happened. Don't you see, Mariella? It all fits now. The Cascade, that we built together. The new job and you. I love you. *You* give me roots. I don't want to be anywhere else. Just with you. You come first, and everything else after that."

She had no words. Never in a million years had she expected such a thing. At her prolonged silence, he spoke again.

"I love you, Mariella. I love you so much it scares the hell out of me."

"No one has ever put me first before."

"Then it's about time, don't you think?" His smile was tender-soft. "You are my center. Nothing else makes sense."

He gripped the arms of her chair. "Living without you frightens me more than risking my heart. The job is mine. Where I live as I'm doing it depends on your answer."

Tears glimmered on her lashes at his heartfelt words. "I could answer, if you asked me a question."

He let go of the chair and stood briefly, reaching into his pocket and then kneeling before her.

"Marry me. Marry me in the ballroom we re-created together, beneath the antique chandelier we found in the attic. Share your life with me. Let us make a home together here. Please say yes."

He held out the ring. There was no doubt in her mind that it was an antique. She stared at the brilliant emerald in the platinum setting, the glitter of inset diamonds on either side.

"It was my grandmother's ring. She said that the emerald was a symbol of love and hope."

She was staggered to see the sheen of moisture in his eyes.

"Don't you see, Mari? That's what you are to me. Love, and hope. Two things I never thought I'd ever have, certainly not together."

"Oh, Luca," she whispered. "I love you so much. And I never believed in happy endings. It certainly never happened for my mother. Perhaps that's why I accepted you leaving as I did. I didn't believe in it. But I have a chance now, to believe, to have faith. And I'd be a fool to let it go."

"Is that a yes?"

"Yes. Yes, yes!"

He gripped her fingers, pulled her to her feet and into his arms.

He stamped a single possessive kiss on her lips before drawing back and sliding the ring over her knuckle.

"Mariella. It is only right that she who carries her name wears her ring. Oh, Mari, what a future we have ahead of us."

Mari touched his face. She was safe with him, body and soul.

"Starting today."

"Starting today," he confirmed, and bent to kiss her again.

* * * * *

*Celebrate 60 years of pure reading pleasure
with Harlequin®!*

*Harlequin Presents® is proud to introduce its
gripping new miniseries,*
THE ROYAL HOUSE OF KAREDES.
*An exquisite coronation diamond, split as a
symbol of a warring royal family's feud, is
missing! But whoever reunites the diamond halves
will rule all....*

*Welcome to eight brand-new titles that unfold to
reveal the stories of kings and queens, princes
and princesses torn apart by pride and power, but
finally reunited by love.*

Step into the world of Karedes with
BILLIONAIRE PRINCE, PREGNANT MISTRESS
*Available July 2009
from Harlequin Presents®.*

ALEXANDROS KAREDES, SNOW DUSTING the shoulders of his leather jacket and glittering like jewels in his dark hair, stood at the door. Maria felt the blood drain from her head.

"Good evening, Ms. Santos."

His voice was as she remembered it. Deep. Husky. Perfect English, but with the faintest hint of a Greek accent. And cold, as cold as it had been that awful morning she would never forget, when he'd accused her of horrible things, called her terrible names....

"Aren't you going to ask me in?"

She fought for composure. Last time they'd faced each other, they'd been on his turf. Now they were on hers. She was in command here, and that meant everything.

"There's a sign on the door downstairs," she said, her tone every bit as frigid as his. "It says, 'No soliciting or vagrants.'"

His lips drew back in a wolfish grin. "Very amusing."

"What do you want, Prince Alexandros?"

A tight smile eased across his mouth and it killed her that even now, knowing he was a vicious, arrogant man, she couldn't help but notice what a handsome mouth it was. Chiseled. Generous. Beautiful, like the rest of him, which made him living proof that beauty could, indeed, be only skin deep.

"Such formality, Maria. You were hardly so proper the last time we were together."

She knew his choice of words was deliberate. She felt her face heat; she couldn't help that but she damned well didn't have to let him lure her into a verbal sparring match.

"I'll ask you once more, your highness. What do you want?"

"Ask me in and I'll tell you."

"I have no intention of asking you in. Tell me why you're here or don't. It's your choice, just as it will be my choice to shut the door in your face."

He laughed. It infuriated her but she could hardly blame him. He was tall—six two, six three—and though he stood with one shoulder leaning against the door frame, hands tucked casually into the pockets of the jacket, his pose was deceptive. He was strong, with the leanly muscled body of a well-trained athlete.

She remembered his body with painful clarity. The feel of him under her hands. The power of him moving over her. The taste of him on her tongue.

Suddenly, he straightened, his laughter gone. "I have not come this distance to stand in your doorway," he said coldly, "and I am not going to leave until I am ready to do so. I suggest you stand aside and stop behaving like a petulant child."

A petulant child? Was that what he thought? This man who had spent hours making love to her and had then accused her of—of trading her body for profit?

Except it had not been love, it had been sex. And the sooner she got rid of him, the better.

She let go of the doorknob and stepped aside. "You have five minutes."

He strolled past her, bringing cold air and the scent of the night with him. She swung toward him, arms folded. He reached past her, pushed the door closed, then folded his arms, too. She wanted to open the door again but she'd be damned if she was going to get into a who's-in-charge-here argument with him. She was in charge, and he would surely see a tussle over the ground rules as a sign of weakness.

Instead, she looked past him at the big clock above her work table.

"Ten seconds gone," she said briskly. "You're wasting time, your highness."

"What I have to say will take longer than five minutes."

"Then you'll just have to learn to economize. More than five minutes, I'll call the police."

Instantly, his hand was wrapped around her wrist.

He tugged her toward him, his dark-chocolate eyes almost black with anger.

"You do that and I'll tell every tabloid shark I can contact about how Maria Santos tried to buy a five-hundred-thousand-dollar commission by seducing a prince." He smiled thinly. "They'll lap it up."

* * * * *

What will it take for this billionaire prince to realize he's falling in love with his mistress…?
Look for
BILLIONAIRE PRINCE, PREGNANT MISTRESS
by Sandra Marton
Available July 2009
from Harlequin Presents®.